MORE PRAISE FOR *THE CONSEQUENCES*

"It's hard to imagine a more gorgeous collection of short fiction."
——Michael Schaub, NPR

"The fact that a mind as fine and compassionate as Muñoz's exists lifts me up." ——George Saunders, *Story Club*

"From deportation fears and the complications of teenage motherhood to the search for belonging and the healing power of kindness, *The Consequences* covers the full breadth of human experience and gives voice to a segment of the population too often stereotyped, taken advantage of or made invisible by our larger society. Simply put, Muñoz's stories are as observant as they are revealing—full of nuanced subtext and bracingly honest depictions of vulnerability and hope, love and regret, and everything in between. They deserve all the attention they can get."
——Alexis Burling, *San Francisco Chronicle*

"In these surprising, vivid stories, worries are deeply felt but not often spoken aloud, and obligation to kin and the need to survive outweigh much else."
——*The Atlantic*, "10 Most Thought-Provoking Books of 2022"

"Muñoz's luminous story collection . . . portrays a community of Mexican and Mexican American farmworkers in California's Central Valley. . . . Their daily difficulties are tenderly laid bare. . . . Muñoz once worked in the same fields, as did his parents and siblings, and his empathetic stories convey a realistic takes on bodies and minds." —Becky

D0905901

"This collection pushes the reader to appreciate life's small moments of unexpected tenderness with fresh eyes."
—Brenda Peynado, *The New York Times Book Review*

"Manuel Muñoz's third story collection solidifies his position as a master of the short story. *The Consequences* offers insights not just into relationships in families, neighborhoods, and communities, but among strangers who meet on a bus and come together to share the struggles of 21st-century immigrant life." —Jane Ciabattari, *Lit Hub*

"Full of nuance and heart, Muñoz's writing is honest and unforgettable, marking him as a master storyteller."
—*Electric Literature*, "Favorite Story Collections of 2022"

"Muñoz brings tenderness and immediacy to these fully realized stories of secrets and concealment, longings, vulnerability, and imperfect escape, creating an expansive and memorable world."
—David Hayden, *The Guardian* (UK)

"This is honest, unsentimental writing, light in touch and delicate in style, but nonetheless unsettling."
—Alison Kelly, *Times Literary Supplement (UK)*

"The characters in Munoz's tough and tender stories play out lives of complicated familial obligations and hard-scrabble economics in the orchards, bus stations, and small apartments of California's Central Valley as summer sizzles and hearts break. . . . There's a glow of warmth as Munoz's compassionate gaze lends grace to these incandescent tales of striving and survival."
—Eithne Farry, *Daily Mail* (UK)

THE CONSEQUENCES

Also by Manuel Muñoz

What You See in the Dark: A Novel
The Faith Healer of Olive Avenue: Stories
Zigzagger: Stories

THE CONSEQUENCES

Stories

Manuel Muñoz

Graywolf Press

"Fantasy and Science Fiction" copyright © 1989 by Rita Dove, from *Collected Poems: 1974–2004* by Rita Dove. Used by permission of W. W. Norton & Company, Inc.

This publication is made possible, in part, by the voters of Minnesota through a Minnesota State Arts Board Operating Support grant, thanks to a legislative appropriation from the arts and cultural heritage fund. Significant support has also been provided by the McKnight Foundation, the Lannan Foundation, the Amazon Literary Partnership, and other generous contributions from foundations, corporations, and individuals. To these organizations and individuals we offer our heartfelt thanks.

MINNESOTA
STATE ARTS BOARD

CLEAN
WATER
LAND &
LEGACY
AMENDMENT

Published by Graywolf Press
212 Third Avenue North, Suite 485
Minneapolis, Minnesota 55401

www.graywolfpress.org

Published in the United States of America

ISBN 978-1-64445-206-6 (paperback)
ISBN 978-1-64445-189-2 (ebook)

4 6 8 10 9 7 5 3

Library of Congress Control Number: 2022930729

Cover design: Carlos Esparza

Cover art: Shutterstock

Este librito es para mi mamá
Esmeralda
y para mi papá
Antonio

Sometimes, shutting a book and rising,
you can walk off the back porch
and into the sea—though
it's not the sort of story
you'd tell your mother.

—*Rita Dove, "Fantasy and Science Fiction"*

CONTENTS

THE CONSEQUENCES

ANYONE CAN DO IT

Her immediate concern was money. It was a Friday when the men didn't come home from the fields and, true, sometimes they wouldn't return until late, the headlights of the neighborhood work truck turning the corner, the men drunk and laughing from the bed of the pickup. And, true, other women might have thought first about the green immigration vans prowling the fields and the orchards all around the Valley, ready to take away the men they might not see again for days if good luck held, or longer if they found no luck at all.

When the street fell silent at dusk, the screen doors of the dark houses opened one by one and the shadows of the women came to sit outside, a vigil on the concrete steps. Delfina was one of them, but her worry was a different sort. She didn't know these women yet and these women didn't know her: she and her husband and her little boy had been in the neighborhood for only a month, renting a two-room house at the end of the street, with a narrow screened-in back porch, a tight bathroom with no insulation, and a mildewed kitchen. There was only a dirt yard for the boy to play in and they had to drive into the town center to use the pay phone to call back to

Delfina not concerned about male safety, but money instead

3

Texas, where Delfina was from. They had been here just long enough for Delfina's husband to be welcomed along to the fieldwork, the pay split among all the neighborhood men, the work truck chugging away from the street before the sun even rose.

When Delfina saw the first silhouette rise in defeat, she thought of the private turmoil these other women felt in the absence of their men, and she knew that her own house held none of that. Just days before the end of June, with the rent due soon, she thought that all the women on the front steps might believe that nothing could be any different until the men returned, that nothing could change until they arrived back from wherever they had been taken. She knew the gravity of her worry, to be sure, but she felt a resolve that seemed absent in the women putting out last cigarettes and retreating behind the screen doors. She watched as the street went dark past sundown and the neighborhood children were sent inside to bed. The longer she held her place on her front steps, the stronger she felt.

From the far end of the street, one of the women emerged from a porch and Delfina saw her walk toward her house, guided by a few dim porch lights and the wan blur of television sets glowing through the windows. When the woman, tall and slender, arrived at her front yard, Delfina could make out the long sleeves of a husband's work shirt and wisps of hair falling from her neighbor's bun. Buenas tardes, the woman said.

Buenas tardes, Delfina answered and, rather than invite her forward, she rose from the steps and met her at the edge of the yard.

Sometimes they don't come back right away, the neighbor said in Spanish. But don't worry. They'll be back soon. All of them. If they take them together, they come back together.

The woman extended her hand. Me llamo Lis, she said.

Delfina, she answered, and as Lis emerged fully out of the street shadow, Delfina saw a face about the same age as hers.

Your house was empty for nearly three months, said Lis, before you arrived. That's a long time around here, even for our neighborhood. Everything costs so much these days.

It does, Delfina agreed.

Was it expensive in Texas? Lis asked. Is that why you moved?

Delfina looked at her placidly, betraying nothing. She had not told this woman that she was from Texas, and she began to wonder what her husband might have said to the other men in the work truck, or in the parking lot of the little corner store near Gold Street, where the owner said nothing about the men's loitering as long as they kept buying beer after a day in the fields.

Your car, Lis said, pointing to the Ford Galaxie parked on the dirt yard. I noticed the Texas license plates when you first came.

We drove it from Texas, Delfina answered.

You're lucky your husband didn't take that car to the fields. They impound them, you know, and it's tough to get them back.

The woman reminded Delfina of her sister back in Texas, who had always tried to talk her into things she didn't want to do. It was her sister who had told her that moving to California was a bad idea, and who had repeated terrible stories about the people who lived there, though she had never been there herself. Her sister had given all the possible reasons why she should stay except for the true one, that she had not wanted to be left alone with their mother.

My husband says they stop you if you don't have California plates, Delfina said. So I try not to drive the car unless I have to.

On the long drive from Texas, she had learned that strangers only introduced themselves when they needed something. She could refuse Lis money if she asked, but it would be hard to deny her a ride into town if she needed it.

Even in the dark, she could tell that Lis was coming up with a response. She had turned her head to look at the Galaxie, her face back in shadow under the streetlight.

I know the farmer, said Lis. We could go out to the orchards and pick up a few rows before he gives all that work away.

I'll have to think about it, said Delfina. My husband doesn't like me driving the car. She remembered what her neighbor had said about impoundment and she tried that: If they take the car . . .

You're from Texas, said Lis, but she pressed no further. Her face was clear and open, but the way she said these words stung, as if being from one side or the other meant anything about how easy or hard things could be. It was none of any stranger's business, but Delfina's husband had never allowed her to work and she knew what women like Lis thought about women like her.

I don't know the first thing about working in the fields anyway, Delfina said. She tried to say it in a way that meant it was the truth and not at all a reply to what Lis had said about Texas.

It's easy but hard at the same time, said Lis. Anyone can do it. It's just that no one really wants to.

I'll have to think about it, said Delfina.

I understand, Lis answered and backed a step out to the street, her arms folded in a way that Delfina recognized from her sister, the way she had stood on the Texas porch in defeat and resignation. Que pases buenas noches, Lis said and began walking away before Delfina had a chance to reply in kind. When she did, she felt her voice carry along the street, as if everyone else on the block had over-heard this refusal, and she went back into the house with an un-expected sense of shame.

Very early the next morning, after a restless night, Delfina woke her little boy from the pallet of blankets on the living room floor. We're going into town, she told him, when Kiki resisted her with grogginess as she struggled to get him dressed. She was about to lead him to the car when she pictured herself driving past Lis's house, how that would look to a woman she had just refused, and her pride took over. She grasped Kiki's hand in her own with such ferocity that

he knew that she meant business and he walked quickly beside her
down the street and around the corner, past the little white church
empty on a Saturday morning and toward town. The boy kept pace
with her somehow and, to her surprise, he made no more protests,
and twenty minutes later, when they reached the TG&Y, she depos-
ited Kiki in the toy aisle without saying a word and marched to the
pay phone at the back of the store to call her mother in Texas.

He left you, her mother's voice said over the line. Nothing keeps
a good father from his family.   ("negative")

They took other men in the neighborhood, too, Delfina said. He
wasn't alone.

How many times did he go out to work here in Texas and he came
home just fine? I told you that you shouldn't have gone. Your sister
was absolutely right . . .

Delfina pulled the phone away from her ear and the vague hec-
toring of her mother barely rippled out along the bolts of fabric and
the sewing notions hanging on the back wall of the store. Delfina
gripped the remaining dimes in her hands, slick and damp in her
palm, and clicked one of them into the phone, the sound cutting out
for a moment as the coin went through.

How's the niño? Is he dreaming about his father yet? That's how
you'll know if he's coming back or not.

Did you hear that? she interrupted her mother, dropping another
coin. I don't have much time left.

Why are you calling? For money? Of course, you're calling for
money. If he's a good father, he'll find a way to send some if he can't
get back.

If you were a good mother, Delfina began, but it came as hardly
even a whisper, and she lacked the courage to talk back this way,
to summon the memory of her white-haired father who had died
years ago and taken with him, it seemed, any criticism of his own
late-night ways. Her voice was lost anyway as her mother yelled out

to turn the phone over to Delfina's sister, and in the moment when the exchange left them all suspended in static, Delfina hung up the receiver. She had not even given them the address for the Western Union office and she would have to apologize, she knew, when the worst of the financial troubles would be upon her. But for the moment, she relished how she had left her older sister calling into the phone, staring back incredulous at her mother.

Come along, she said to Kiki, when she went to collect him from the toy aisle, where he had quietly scattered the pieces of a board game without the notice of the clerk. He started to cry out in protest, now that he was in the cool and quiet of the five-and-dime and she was pulling him away from the bins of marbles and plastic army men. Delfina imagined the footsteps of the clerk coming to check on the commotion and, in her hurry to shove the board game back onto the shelf, she let slip the pay phone dimes, Kiki frozen in surprise by their clatter before he stooped to pick them up.

Come along, she said again, letting him have the dimes. Ice cream, she whispered in encouragement, and led on by this suggestion, he followed her out of the store. Kiki fell meek and quiet once again, as if he knew not to jeopardize his sudden fortune. It was only right to reward him with the promised treat and she led him down the street to the drugstore with its ice cream counter visible from the large front window. It was only ten in the morning and the young woman at the main register had to come around to serve them two single scoops, but Delfina didn't even take the money from Kiki's hands to pay for it. She had a single folded dollar bill in her pocket and she handed it to the clerk, foolish, she thought, to be spending so frivolously. But her boy didn't need to know those troubles. His Saturday was coming along like any other, his father sometimes not home at sundown and always gone at sunrise. There was no reason to get him wondering about things he wasn't yet wondering about.

Delfina led him to the little park across the street from the town bank. He gripped his cone tightly and his other hand held the fist of dimes. She motioned him to pocket the change for safekeeping. Put it away, she said, sitting on one of the benches. But her little boy kept them in his grip and so she patted his pocket more firmly to encourage him and that's when she felt it, a hard little object that she knew instantly was something he had stolen from the toy aisle. → her son steals, uh oh

Let me see, she said, or I will take away your coins. Kiki struggled against her, smearing some of the ice cream on his pants, which finally distressed him enough into actual tears. Ya, ya, Delfina said, calming him, and fished out what was in his pocket, a little green car, metal and surprisingly heavy. Her little boy was inconsolable and the Saturday shoppers along the sidewalk stopped to look in their direction. Sssh, she told him, there, there, and took the time to show him the car in the palm of her hand before she slipped it back into his pocket. Ya, ya, she said one more time, and leaned back on the bench, the Saturday morning going by.

Later, when they rounded the corner back into the neighborhood, she saw Lis out in her dirt yard. She was tending to a small bed of wild sunflowers, weeding around them with a hoe, her back turned to the street. The closer they got to Lis's yard, the harder the scuffling of Kiki's shoes became and Lis turned around toward the noise.

Buenos días, Delfina greeted her. She wanted to keep walking but Lis made her way toward her and she knew she would have to stop and listen, much like the time in Arizona on the trip out here, when she had accidently locked eyes with a man at a gas station, and he had walked over to rap on the window of the Galaxie and beg for some change.

Good thing we didn't go to the orchards after all, said Lis. I would've felt terrible if your car had stalled out there.

No . . . Delfina began. I . . . The more she stumbled, the less it made sense to make up any story at all. There was no reason to be anything but honest.

The car is fine, she said. I just wanted him to walk a bit. We got ice cream.

For breakfast, Lis said, looking down at Kiki and smiling. What a Saturday! The morning's sweat matted her hair down on her forehead and she wore no gloves, her fingers a bit raw from the metal handle of the hoe, but she was cheerful with Kiki, recognizing his exhaustion. Her daughter, Delfina realized, was not out helping her, but inside the cool of the house, and she took this as a sign of the same propensity for sacrifice that she believed herself to hold.

I've thought about it, Delfina said, though she really hadn't. I think it's a good idea.

I'm glad, said Lis.

I wish I had said so last night. We could've put in a day's work. But I'm happy to go tomorrow.

Tomorrow's Sunday, said Lis, and when Delfina put her hand up to her mouth as if she'd forgotten, as if she might change her mind, Lis moved even closer to her, looking down at Kiki. But work never waits, she said.

El día de Dios, said Delfina. I didn't even think of it.

People work, said Lis. Don't worry about it.

We can wait until Monday. That way the children can be at school.

Like I told you, my daughter is old enough to watch him, if you trust her. I leave her alone sometimes. Or we can bring them out with us and stay longer.

Delfina could make out the shadow of a child watching from behind the screen door and, catching her glance past her shoulder, Lis turned to look. She called her forth and her daughter stepped out, a girl very tall for ten years old. This is our neighbor, Lis explained, and we'll need you to watch her little boy tomorrow. Will you do that?

The girl nodded and she stuck out her hand to Delfina in awkward politeness.

What's your name? Delfina asked.

Irma, the girl said, very quietly, her voice deferential. She had small eyes that she squinted as if in embarrassment and Delfina wondered if she knew she needed glasses but was too afraid to say.

We can trust you, can't we, said Lis, to take care of the little boy? If I leave you some food, you can feed him, can't you?

Oh, I can leave them something . . .

Don't worry, said Lis. I can leave something easy to fix and you can bring out something for us in the orchard. I have a little ice chest to keep everything out of the sun.

After Delfina nodded her head in agreement, Lis made as if to go back to her yard work. At dawn, then, Lis said. I'll bring everything we need.

For the rest of the day, Delfina was restless, anxious that every noise on the street might signal the return of the men. To have them come back would mean the lull of normalcy, of what had been and would continue to be, just when she was on the brink of doing something truly on her own. But the street stayed quiet. The afternoon heat swallowed the houses and by evening, some of the shadows resumed their evening watch, sitting stiffly but without much hope or expectation. They turned back in before night had fully come and Delfina went to bed early, too.

At dawn, she roused Kiki from the blankets strewn on the living room floor and poured him some cereal. He blinked against the harshness of the kitchen light at such an early hour, surprised at his mother wearing one of his father's long-sleeved work shirts, and even more surprised by the knock at the door. Lis stood there, her daughter behind her. Buenos días, Delfina said and waved the girl Irma inside. She poured her a bowl of cereal, too, and Irma sat quietly at the table without having to be told to do so.

Thank you for taking care of him, Delfina said. We'll be back in the middle of the afternoon. She knew she didn't have to say more than that, trusted that Lis had spoken with the same motherly sense of warning that she used. Still, it was only now, on the brink of leaving them alone for the day, that she wished she had asked Kiki if he had been dreaming about his father, if he might have communicated something about what was true for him while he slept.

Lis showed her the gloves and the work knives and then the two costales to hold the fruit, a sturdy one of thick canvas with a hearty shoulder strap and a smaller one of nylon mesh. Her other hand balanced a water jug and a small ice chest, where Delfina put in a bundle of foil-wrapped bean tacos that would keep through the heat of the day.

In the car, Lis pointed her south of town and toward the orchards and Delfina drove along. They kept going south, the orchards endless, cars parked over on the side of the road and pickers approaching foremen, work already getting started even though the dawn's light hadn't yet seeped into the trees.

Up there, Lis said, where a few cars had already lined up and several workers had gathered around a man sitting on the open tailgate of his work truck. Wait here, she said.

Before Delfina could ask why, Lis had exited, approaching the man with a handshake. He seemed to recognize her and then looked back at Delfina in the car. Lis finished what she had needed to say and the man took one more look at Delfina and then pointed down the rows.

Lis motioned her to get out of the car.

He says he'll give us two rows for now and we do what we can. If we're fast, he'll give us more. And he's letting us use a ladder free of charge.

That's kind of him . . .

They charge sometimes, Lis said. She took one end of a heavy-looking wooden ladder, the tripod hinge rusty and the rungs worn smooth in the middle. So fifty-fifty?

Half and half, Delfina agreed.

I can pick the tops and you can do the bottoms, if you're afraid of heights. Or you can walk the costales back to the crates for weighing. Give them your name if you want to, but make sure the foreman tells you exactly how much we brought in.

They worked quickly, the morning still cool. Delfina parted the leaves where the peaches sat golden among the boughs and the work felt easy at first. The fruit came down with scarcely more than a tug and when she yanked hard enough to rustle the branches, Lis spoke her advice from the ladder above. Just the redder ones and not too hard. Feel them, she said. If they're too hard, leave them. Someone else will come back around in a few days and they'll be riper then.

They did a few rounds like this, Delfina taking the costales back to the road to have them weighed. Sometimes Lis was ready with the smaller nylon sack and sometimes Delfina had to wait for other pickers to have their fruit accounted for. The morning moved on, a brighter white light coming into the orchard as they got closer to noon. As they picked the trees near clean, they moved deeper and deeper into the orchard and the walk back to the crates took longer, Lis almost lost to her among the leaves.

They had not quite finished the row when the sun finally peaked directly overhead and their end of the orchard sank into quiet. Delfina let out a sigh upon her return.

I should've brought the ice chest while I was there.

I can get it, said Lis. You've walked enough. She came down with the half-empty nylon costal and pulled a few more peaches from the bottom boughs while Delfina rested. She started walking toward the road, then turned around. The keys, she said, and held out her hand.

Delfina watched her go. Lis walked quickly with the nylon costal dangling over her shoulder. Maybe the weight of Lis's work was all in her arms from stretching and pulling, and not heavy and burning in the thighs like hers. Delfina took a peach for herself, the plumpest she could reach without stretching, and sat in the higher bank of the orchard row, catching her breath, massaging her upper legs and resting. It was a Sunday, she remembered, and Lis had been right after all. People did work on this day, even if it felt as tranquil and lonely as Sundays always did, here among the trees with the leaves growing more and more still, the orchard quiet and then quieter. Sundays were always so peaceful, Delfina thought, no matter where you were, so serene she imagined the birds themselves had gone dumb. El día de Dios, she thought, and remembered Sundays when her white-haired father had not yet slept out the drunkenness of the previous night. Her own husband had sometimes broken the sacredness of a Sunday silence and she was oddly thankful for the calm of this orchard moment that had been brought on only by his absence. Delfina ate the last bits of her peach and tossed the pit into the dirt, looking down the row to soak in that blessed quiet. The longer she looked, the emptier and emptier it became. The empty row where, she realized, Lis had disappeared like a faraway star.

She started back toward the road. The walk was long and she couldn't hear a sound, not of the other workers, not other cars rumbling past the orchards, just the endless trees and her feet against the heavy dirt of the fields. The day's weariness slowed her and made the trees impossible to count, but she walked on, resolute, the gray of the road coming into view. She emerged onto the shoulder of the road and saw the foreman and the foreman's truck and a few other cars, but the Galaxie was gone.

Excuse me, she said, approaching the foreman, who seemed surprised to see her, though he had seen her all morning, noting down the weight of the peaches she had brought in, saying the numbers twice, tallied under the last name Arellano.

You're still here, the foreman said, very kindly, as if the fact was

[handwritten marginal note: almost thankful to be free of men]

a surprise to him too, and his face grew into a scowl like the faces of the white men Delfina had encountered in Texas, the ones who always seemed surprised that she spoke English. But where their faces had been steely and uncaring, his softened with concern, as if he recognized that he had made a serious mistake.

I thought you were gone . . . he said.

We were supposed to split . . . She held a hand to her head and looked up the road, one way and then the other, as if the car were on its way back, Lis having gone only to the small country store to fetch colder drinks.

Arellano, the foreman said, tapping his ledger. Arellano is the first name on the list, he said. I paid it out about a half hour ago.

That was my car, Delfina said, as if that would be enough for him to know what to do next. But the foreman only stared back at her. It was my husband's car, she said, because that was how she saw it now, what her husband would say about its loss if he ever made it back.

She told me that you two were sisters, the foreman said. If he only knew, Delfina thought, her real sister back in Texas. The mere mention made her turn back toward the orchard and walk into the row. She could sense the foreman walking to the row's opening to see where she was going, and when she reached the ladder, she folded it down and heaved it best as she could, its legs cutting a little trough behind her as she dragged it back to the road.

You didn't have to do that, the foreman said.

You did right by letting us use it, Delfina said. It's only fair. Other pickers had approached the foreman's truck and he attended to them, though he kept looking over at Delfina now and then, his face sunken in concern. None of the workers looked at her and she let go of the idea of asking any of them for a ride back into town. She sat in the dirt under the shade of a peach tree and watched while the foreman flipped out small wads of cash as the workers began to quit

for the afternoon. When the last of them shook hands with the foreman and began to leave, she rose to help him load all of the wooden
ladders back on to the truck.

He accepted her help and opened the door of the truck cab, motioning for her to get in. They drove slowly back into town, the ladders clattering with every stop and start, the weight of them shifting
and settling. Neither of them said a word, but before the orchards
gave way back to the houses, the foreman cleared his throat and
spoke: I think it's the first time I ever had two women come out
alone like that, but I was raised to think that anybody can do anything and you don't ask questions just because something isn't normal. Even just a little bit of work is better than none at all and I kept
thinking about the story she told me, that you two were sisters and
that your husbands had gotten thrown over the border. You can tell
a lot by a wife who wants to work as hard as her husband, you know
what I mean? I wasn't sure you could finish two rows just the both
of you, but you kept coming and coming with those sacks and that's
how I knew you had kids to feed.

At the four-way intersection, just before the last mile into town,
the foreman fished into his pocket and pulled out a bill. Take it, he
said. He handed it to her, a twenty, and almost pushed it into Delfina's
hands as he started the turn, needing to keep the steering wheel
steady. The bill fluttered in her fingers from the breeze of the open
passenger window, but the truck wasn't going to pick up much more
speed. She wouldn't lose it.

Thank you, she said.

It's not your fault, he said. And I'm not defending her for what
she did. But I believe any story that anybody tells me. You can't be to
blame if you got faith in people.

You're right, she agreed. And though she didn't have to say it, she
followed it with the words of blind acceptance before she could stop

they were protective over their kids

not she's speaking her mind

herself. I understand, she said, and it was not worth explaining that she really didn't.

Where should I take you? asked the foreman.

She didn't hesitate. There's a little store right near Gold Street, just across the tracks, she said. If you could stop, just so I can get something for my boy.

Of course, he said, though there could have been no other possible way to respond, since Delfina's request came with a small hiccup of tears, which she quickly swallowed away as the truck pulled into the store's small lot. Other workers had stopped there, too, and men from other neighborhoods lingered out front with their open cases of beer and skinny bags of sunflower seeds, staring at her as she wiped at her face with her dirty sleeves. She brought a package of bologna and a loaf of bread to the register and fished out three bottles of cola from the case at the front counter. The clerk broke the twenty into a bundle of ones, and she held them with the temporary solace of pretending there would be money enough for the days ahead and that money was going to be the least of her worries anyway.

She directed the foreman just a couple more blocks and when they turned the corner, the neighborhood held a Sunday quiet that made her think first of an empty church, but she had not been to a service in years. No, it was a quiet like the porch of the house in Texas when she and her husband had driven away, leaving her sister and her mother, a stillness that she was sure held only so long before one of them had started crying, followed by the other. A calm like that could only be broken by the bereft and that was how she understood that neither of them would ever forgive her. But that didn't matter now. The hotter days of July were coming, Delfina knew, and the work of picking all the fruit would last from sunup to sundown. Something would work out, she told herself, clear and resolute against the emptiness of her neighborhood, Lis's house stark in

This woman stole her car & took away the kids protector

its vacancy. There, she said, pointing to her house, and she wasn't surprised to see Kiki sitting there on the front steps all alone.

There he is, waiting for his mama, the foreman said, as he pulled
up, and Kiki looked back at them, with neither curiosity nor glee.

She handed the foreman the third cola bottle.

You know, he said, it'll work out in the end. Sisters always end up
doing the right thing. She'll be back, you'll see.

What story had he figured out for himself, Delfina wondered,
after she hadn't bothered to correct him about Lis not being her sister, and she decided that this also mattered little in the end, how he
would explain this to his wife back home. She would not explain
this to her husband when he came back. All her husband would care
about was what happened to the Galaxie and that would be enough
of a story. She might even tell her husband about the luck of the
twenty-dollar bill but she would hold private the detail of the ring
on the foreman's finger. She would hold in her mind what it felt like
to be treated with a faithful kindness.

Thank you, she said, and descended from the truck cab, nodding
her head goodbye.

On the steps, Kiki eyed the tall bottles of cola in her hand. But
first there was the heavy field dust to pound away from her shoes and
the tiredness she could suddenly feel in her bones. Delfina kicked
her shoes off and sat on the front steps. She lodged one of the bottles
under the water spigot to pop the cap, a trick she had seen her husband do. She handed that bottle to Kiki and he took it with both
hands, full of thirst or greed for the sweetness, she couldn't tell. She
took some of the bread loaf and the bologna for herself and offered
him a bite, knowing he wouldn't eat one of his own. He was hungry and this was how she knew that Irma was gone, too. She was a
girl who did what she was told and Delfina didn't blame her. Kiki
crowded close to her knees, even in the heat of the afternoon, and
so she popped the cap of the second bottle to take a sip herself and to

ask her little boy of no words to tell where he thought the older girl had gone, of where he dreamed his father was. Dígame, she said, asking him to tell her a whole story, but Kiki had already taken the little metal car from his pocket and he was showing her, starting from the crook of his arm, how a car had driven away slowly, slowly, and on out past the edge of his little hand and out of their lives forever.

THE HAPPIEST GIRL IN
THE WHOLE USA

Timoteo really is nothing special, shorter than me and rounder, and hardly even a smile to break the dark moon of his face. I say no one special because it is still, after all these years, just me and him. No one special because I'm no different from any of the women who line up at the town bank, ready to exchange my saved collection of coins for a wad of sweaty bills. It takes money to get a man back from the border, more money than most might think.

Some of us have rings on our fingers and some of us don't, but we all know what it means to watch the calendar turn to the last of the month. We know what some of the farmers do on final Fridays, and we know what to do on Saturday mornings. The farmers put their dusty hands on a phone receiver and very calmly place a call to the migra. Then the men in the green uniforms arrive at the rows of what-ever crops are in season—grapes or peaches or plums—and round up the men into vans. No one ends up paid for the week's labor, and everyone gets a standard booking in either Visalia or Fresno before being hustled back onto the vehicles. By nighttime, the vans reach

Bakersfield and start the slow ascent into the mountains. They will head through Los Angeles—where all our men know it's easy to get lost, but expensive to live—then on to San Diego, where it's just expensive to live. Finally, they'll reach the border itself and Tijuana, where the van doors open to let all of the men out so they can start over again.

The bank teller counts out the bills as quickly as she can. She is a very pretty white girl who always wears skirts, her hair pulled up with simple barrettes. She knows the bus from Fresno stops once a week in our town now, Saturday midafternoon in front of the barber shop, as if the whole drama of deportation and return was a big plan between the migra and the charter companies. She hurries, and though she never says much of a pleasant word to any of us, I think it is because she doesn't want us to miss the only bus going out of town, the only way to get our men back. I often wonder about the history of her good luck. I don't always know what to think of the fact that she doesn't have a ring on her finger, if it is a good or a bad thing.

It's always the same when I board the bus—it's already half-full, mostly women from Fresno and the little towns just south of it, like Fowler and Selma. I get a seat alone and the bus moves on to Goshen, then Tulare and Delano, each woman who boards more weary than the last. They're all like me. Or at least, they look like me. I don't know their histories. I don't know if they came from south Texas like I did, were taken from school in the third grade to work in the fields like me. I was resentful of my parents for giving me the life of a dumb mule and I left them almost to the minute of my eighteenth birthday, with only a scrap of paper with their address and phone number that I never ended up using. I walk around with a lot of pride because I did that, because I proved that I could support myself in a hard world. I did all right for myself for a while. Then I fell in love.

When we get to Bakersfield, the bus is packed, and a young woman boards with a big sigh and looks at the seat beside me.

Con permiso, she says, before she moves to sit down.

I know just from looking at her that this is her first trip. She carries a cheap white purse in one hand and a bulky shopping bag in the other. She reminds me of all the women in town who everybody knows have just recently arrived from Mexico, because they go to the grocery store in high heels and tight dresses, doing their best to be like the American women they see on television.

She's wearing a purple dress and white high heels, and just by that I know she spends too much time watching the afternoon soap operas, not understanding that the women on those shows only scheme because they have no jobs to go to. It will take a while for her to someday let the TV station rest on the evening news with Jessica Savitch—the kind of person I wish I was smart enough to sound like—when the need to listen to English for practice turns into a wish to look like an intelligent and confident woman.

She sits down quickly as the bus begins to pull out of the station, and when she adjusts the shopping bag under her legs, I look at her hands, but there isn't a ring to be found.

The bus is back on the road and, soon enough, I can feel the rise into the mountains, the ascent into Los Angeles. My stomach flutters like the times when Timoteo and I boarded the cheap traveling carnival rides that sometimes set up in the town park, and I place my hand on my ribs, remembering.

Are you hungry? the young girl says to me in Spanish.

I didn't know she had been looking at me, and before I can answer, she reaches into the shopping bag and brings out something wrapped in foil. When I don't take it immediately, she begins to unwrap it—a taco of corn tortilla and something orange—and tears off a piece for herself.

Take it, she says, handing me the part still in the foil. It's cold, but delicious: chorizo and potato. I nod my thanks. Where are you headed? she asks.

Los Angeles, I answer. I think to ask where she might be headed but I already know.

She says nothing for a moment, and just when I feel bad that I haven't asked her a question, she finishes her food and carefully pulls a tissue from her bra to wipe her fingers. Do you know Los Angeles very well? she asks.

What do you mean?

Do you know the city? Do you know your way around?

I know some places. Around the bus station, I mean.

She dabs at her lips with the tissue before balling it into her fist. Would you help me when we get there?

Help you how?

She reaches for her cheap white purse and pulls out a folded piece of paper.

The bus has darkened with the coming of sundown and the road's curve into the high walls of the mountains. She shows me the paper—a map—in the bare light.

He told me to look for the park, she says.

I know the park and I know the agreed routine: Pershing Square, where I know to wait overnight to see if Timoteo might show up from Tijuana, spending a night at a motel near Seventh Street where the door opens out to the city's loud darkness. If Timoteo doesn't show, then I know to board the bus to San Diego, this time to the bus station almost within sight of the border, as if both countries wanted to make everything easier on everyone. Nearby is a park just like the one in Los Angeles, where everyone waits and waits and waits.

If I don't show up there, Timoteo always tells me, then you know it's over.

I know that park, I say to her. It's very close by.

Would you mind showing me?

[handwritten marginal note:] the plan to get illegal documentation?.

Of course, I say, but maybe I don't say it with much conviction.

No, really, she says. I don't know where I'm going. I've never had to stop in Los Angeles, and it's a scary city.

It's big, but not scary when you get used to it.

You've been there a lot? When did you cross over?

"I was born here," I tell her in English, then I say it again to her in Spanish, then I let her stay silent for a moment so she can know who she's talking to. To me, she's a young girl without a name. She's someone who might not have anything in her purse except the folded-up map, who might not know how much money to take on a trip like this.

I take the map from her hand. Who are you going to see? I ask and tilt the paper toward the fading light of the bus window, following the map with my clean finger. She doesn't answer.

You don't have to be married to be in love, I tell her. I understand.

She leans her head toward me, as if to study the map together. But there's nothing to study. The street is a straight shot from the bus station to the park, but I trace its path for her with my finger.

When we get off at the station, a lot of people will head here, along this street, over to the park, I say. It's a long walk in the dark, but if you stay close to the group you can feel safe. You can take a taxi if you want to, but I think it's a waste of money. And sometimes the drivers circle around just to cheat you, so be careful.

Thank you— she says to me and I can tell by how she says it that she wants to insist, one more time, that I show her. But I meant to say *we* and *a lot of people* and *stay close* to let her know that she should just follow everyone, all of us on the same trip, the same type of man at the other end. She's too young to understand though.

My name is Natalia, she says.

Good to meet you, I tell Natalia. The bus has gone dark and I can feel some of the gradual descent toward Los Angeles, so I lean my head against the window. I close my eyes as if to nap, but I don't offer my name.

She's quiet while I pretend to nap and with my eyes closed, I think back to a Natalia I knew back in south Texas, one of two other girls in my third-grade class. They were good friends to me, both of them, Natalia and the other one, and we sat in the last row of the classroom while the rowdy boys tried to impress the teacher. I remember third grade because it was the last year I ever had in school. I was a smart girl, smarter than the boys, and I was filled with a need to prove myself better than them. One day, our teacher asked the class a simple question. Which weighed more, a pound of feathers or a pound of gold? The boys went out of their way to explain why one would be heavier than the other, until I finally raised my hand. When the teacher called on me, I said, without hesitation, A pound is a pound, no matter what.

On the bus, I open my eyes again to the silence I remember from the classroom. In the dark, all the women are sleeping, this new Natalia next to me, not the same girl, but the same thinking: Latch on to someone who can move around in the world, someone who can help you. I can't imagine whatever happened to those girlhood friends, if they ever got out of south Texas, but I remember they were sweet to me after the teacher opened the top drawer of her desk, then came down the aisle with a white ribbon in her hand. The room went silent, almost dark, from everyone's watching, and the teacher placed the ribbon in front of me. *Do something with your life, Griselda.*

When we arrive at the station, I have to goad Natalia ahead so we can get off the bus. She stands so bewildered with her two bags at the rush of the station that it's all I can do to not take her hand in mine. Come, I tell her, as a group of our fellow passengers makes its way to the exit, and she follows me through the grimy bustle of the station, the sleepy eyes, the baby strollers, the impatience. The better part of me says I should turn around to make sure she is close behind, that she hasn't been swallowed up by what is, for her, the surprise of so many people at nine in the evening. I don't ask if she's hungry or if she'd like a drink or if she needs the restroom—there is never time for anything on a trip like this—and she follows me past the coffee-dispensing machines, the bank of pay phones, the ticket counters with their long lines of arguments. We follow the other passengers who had been on the bus, all of us a flock of birds swerving onto the street.

Natalia is having trouble keeping up. She's figured out that her white shoes are not made for walking, but I tell her nothing about the stupidity of wearing a dress. She should be smart enough for this world on her own, I think to myself, for the day that demands she do this trip alone with no one to help her. I can hear the click-click of her heels along the sidewalk, so I know she's behind me. The sweat on my brow appears quickly; sometimes, the Los Angeles nights are balmy and bearable, but tonight it feels as if we brought the Valley heat with us. I can hear her breathing heavily behind me, but I do not turn around. We hardly need the other passengers as our guides anymore. We're walking quickly enough to show we are determined, not lost or tired, and our pace blends us into the life on the sidewalk: the late-shift weekend workers waiting at the city bus benches; the exhaust of the taxicabs idling at the corners; boys on bikes who are too young to be out so late; the hot fluorescence of a tiendita, its vegetables wilting in the heat.

How much further? Natalia finally says, and when I turn around, I can see the sweat stains in dark circles under her arms, how hard she tries to not show a slight limp in her right foot, a blister no doubt.

Two more blocks, I tell her. The other passengers—we were never really a group at all—have long since reached the park, fanning out to look for their men. Not once along the way were we spoken to or looked at, the street always humming with traffic, inviting what I know is a false sense of safety.

Will you remember the way back to the station?

Yes, she says, looking around, and she says it so confidently that I have to believe her, even though I wonder about the man who she is coming to meet, if he would lead her by the hand back to the station. She says it so confidently that I know immediately that it has never occurred to her that her man might not have made it to the park to begin with.

That's when I know she is truly lost.

Come, I tell her again, when we reach the edge of the park, and here, I know, is where her eyes will be opened, where she'll learn to never again wear a purple dress on such a trip. Stay with me, I tell her as we approach the benches filled with men in T-shirts so white they glow in the dark, all of them waiting. I don't call out Timoteo's name—I learned a long time ago never to do that—and Natalia's fear gets the better of her. She stays silent as we near the benches, close enough to the small groups to make out faces, sometimes a cigarette lighter briefly illuminating a circle of tired, anxious men. Mamasita, I hear someone mutter, and the single word is followed by the ugly laughter of too many men to count. ¿Dónde me llevas? says another one, and Natalia takes my hand out of sheer fright, her grip tighter than mine. If she wore a ring, it would have dug into me.

We circle the park twice, then cut across it once, but Timoteo is not in any of the usual spots. I stand looking back at the darkness, thinking about whether I should go back in or give it another hour. But I know Timoteo has not made it to Los Angeles tonight, and that I need to board the bus in the morning and head to San Diego.

What do we do now? Natalia asks. He said he would be here.

It's hard, I tell her. You remember.

I have done this so many times that Timoteo's failure to show up at the park only means I have to spend more money to get him back home. But for Natalia, I know, it means her hand-drawn map is useless, as if she were standing not at a park entrance, but at the edge of the world.

What do we do now? she asks again. She looks at the dark park and, in the dim streetlight, I think I can see tears forming in her eyes. He said he would be here.

Things happen, I tell her. Did you bring any money? I ask her, keeping my voice low. For a motel?

He said he would be here . . . she says, trailing off.

Despite everything, I am a smart person in the world. I could have been even smarter and better if life had turned out a certain way. If I could have stayed in school, there may have been more than just white ribbons. I think of the young Natalia from my girl days and I take this one's hands, and then the name of the other girl comes to me—Carla!—as if her spirit knew that someone had been thinking of her. Such sweet girls, wherever they wound up.

[handwritten marginal note: he thinks he would've been even smarter if he stayed in school]

Come with me, I tell her, and we turn and walk back in the direction of the station. Natalia follows me without a word, and I eventually take a left toward the motel I always stay at when I need to. But first, I direct Natalia into the corner tiendita just out of eyeshot of the motel office. Go in there and pretend to look at the vegetables, I tell her, and her eyes widen, her hands stiff around my wrist when she realizes I am about to leave her. No, I tell her. The motel charges per person.

Please don't leave me, she says.

I promise, I tell her, and I know I don't say it with much kindness in my voice. But I don't rush away and I don't turn back to look at her. If she chooses to follow me to the motel instead of waiting, I won't pay the extra lodging fee to keep her safe. If Natalia chooses to leave the safety of the tiendita, then she's on her own.

With the key secure in my hand, I walk back to the tiendita and find her cradling a box of saltines and two tins of Vienna sausages. I know the packaged sandwiches—salty ham and American cheese—are half off at night, so I get one and a tall bottle of soda. When I place them on the counter, I tell the clerk, Just these, to see if Natalia can fish any money out of her purse.

I'll wait for you outside, I tell her, as she counts out change to the clerk and waits for him to bag her items. When she click-clicks her way back out to the sidewalk, everything is set, and I know she'll be with me for the rest of the night and a good part of the morning.

Now listen, I tell her. Just stay a little ways behind me on the other side of the street, and don't cross until you pass the main office window. If the owner thinks we're together, it's going to cost me.

I give her the room number and point to where we're headed, her heels so faint in the night I think for a moment that I've already lost her. I could've done the right thing and taken one of her bags, but then she'd never learn how to travel with hardly anything.

I go into the motel room and set my dinner on the table with the television, leaving the door slightly ajar and the light off. Her heels gradually click-click from across the street and into the parking lot, a greater racket than I thought, and I wave at her to rush quickly to the door. She slips in and when I close the door behind her, I do so as quietly as I can, hesitating to turn on the light. When I finally let out a sigh of relief and slip the lock on, she hears my frustration.

I'm sorry, she says.

I turn on the light. Keep your voice down, I say and open my paper bag from the tiendita. Let's eat.

She kicks off her white high heels and rubs her feet while I eat my sandwich. I can see the red patches where blisters will appear in the morning. Eat, I tell her. We need to be up early.

I'm surprised when she doesn't open the Vienna sausage tins or the saltines, but takes out her last two cold tacos, as if standing in the glare of the tiendita taught her that the only food she should ever bring along is the kind that can keep.

I don't have any money— Natalia starts.

I had to spend it on a room anyway, I tell her. But tomorrow, you're on your own. The moment I say it, the words sound cruel, but there is no way to explain to her what self-reliance means without bringing up the past. She doesn't need to know my past. She doesn't even know my name.

You're lucky, I tell her. Sometimes people are not kind. Especially other women who are by themselves.

I hope my luck doesn't run out tomorrow.

He'll show up, I say, but he may not, and the better part of me is already thinking ahead, to the kind of person I am if Timoteo shows up in the morning and I go back to my life by forgetting about her.

So why aren't you married? I ask her. I'm looking at her hands again, her fingers, and thinking about the man she's come to get.

I want to get married, Natalia answers. But I have to wait for him to ask.

Do you have children?

No, she says. Not yet.

You better marry him, I say, hearing the longing in her voice, knowing how much harder it will be if he saddles her with his children before disappearing.

But you're not married.

So she noticed my bare hands, too.

He's too afraid to marry me.

Men are always afraid.

No, I say. He's not afraid of marriage. I'm a citizen. I've been telling him for years that marriage would solve a lot of our problems. When he asks me what we have to do, I tell him we have to go to city hall and get a license, and that's when he gets afraid. Like a lot of people, he's scared of the government.

Everyone should be afraid of the government.

Maybe in Mexico, I tell her. But I was born here and I don't let anybody push me around. ` somewhat of a superiority complex

Natalia looks at me as if this revelation is beyond belief. She puts down the last bite of her taco and smoothes the empty shopping bag flat against the little table. I can see from her face that a wave of relief has crossed it, that my determination comes from a place she can name, maybe even get to. I think again of the young Natalia from my girl days and Carla, too, and wonder if it would have made a difference if someone had told us more about the world.

I was born in Texas, I tell her. I went to school for a little bit. That's how I know English. For once, this means something, and all the despair I've ever had about being no better off than where I came from dims in the light of Natalia's silence, the futility of her white shoes and her purple dress, with no one in this new world to show her how to survive.

Eat, I tell her, motioning to the last bite. My sandwich is almost gone, the soda flat and warm, and as soon as I take the last mouthful, I know I'm going to rise and prepare for bed. I look down at Natalia's reddened feet. We have the same shoe size, I bet.

You think so?

I lean down and hand her my sneaker. Try it on, I urge her. When it fits her like a glove, I get up from the chair and go to the bathroom, taking off my socks. I turn on the water and plug the sink. Why don't you wear the sneakers tomorrow? I tell her, dipping the socks in the water and unwrapping the motel soap to wash them for her. She's silent in the next room, maybe with the sneaker still on her single foot, maybe with the taco unfinished on the table, but she can hear my determination in the splashing of the water and the soap. Natalia must be no more than nineteen or twenty years old. Even if her man shows up, I know he won't be much to worry over. It's not my place to correct her mistake in placing so much trust in one man, but at least I can see that she knows how to spot the resilience in another woman and learn from it, like my two schoolyard friends, the little Natalia, the little Carla, wherever my poor girls ended up.

I close the bathroom door to wash up and prepare for bed, hang the socks to dry. On any other night, I could take off my bra and panties to wash in the sink and dry overnight, sleep in some comfort, but I would be a fool to trust Natalia completely. Now I'll have to hide the money in one of the bra cups, safe next to me once I drift off, dead tired. My panties are tattered—I don't have to impress Timoteo anymore—but I hate that I'll have to wear them two days in a row without washing.

We need to sleep soon, I say, when I walk back out, and Natalia complies. She tidies the table and washes up in the bathroom, but when she emerges, she still has her purple dress on. She crosses the room to turn out the light before she undresses, and the darkness amplifies the street noise of late-night Los Angeles, the far-off sirens, men's voices faint on the street, always sinister no matter what they might be talking about. Natalia takes her side of the bed and doesn't move for the longest time, but I can tell by her breathing that she can't sleep, that's she afraid of tomorrow.

I can't sleep either, not sure of what to do in the morning. I don't toss around, though. I stay rigid in bed, thinking of my old stern teacher from south Texas, the way she walked down the row of desks with her back straight. She walked with determination. She walked as if everything in her life had gone as planned. Her face comes to me, clearer and clearer, the white ribbon in her hand, and when my eyes finally close, her name comes to me—Mrs. Rolnik—and almost as suddenly, I can see the faint gray light of the morning through the ugly mustard-colored drapes.

Timoteo will be there this morning. I know it in my bones. I rouse Natalia and tell her to shower, and while she's in the bathroom, I take out the motel's pen and paper from the nightstand and write my own name and phone number and address. I do it because Timoteo will come back—he always does—and I do it because everyone needs someone in this world. I take just enough bills to cover either a bus ticket back home or another night in the motel and I pray to the god I don't believe in that she'll make the right decision.

Natalia emerges from the bathroom in a lime-green dress, the same style as the purple one, which tells me she knows a good bargain. Later, she'll understand that it means little to suffer the indignity of wearing the same clothes two or three days in a row. When we're ready, I send her across the street ahead of me while I go to turn in the key. She walks briskly now that she's wearing the sneakers, but the socks weren't dry yet. I'll have to remind her to take them off for a moment when we sit at the park, let them air out in the sunlight. I have to cuff my jeans so the hems won't stick on the heels of her white shoes and when I click-click along to the motel office, key in hand, the sound betrays her ridiculous wish to be the white women on the soap operas, at the county offices, at the JCPenney.

Los Angeles is different in the daytime, but it is Sunday morning just like everywhere else, quiet, just a few cars on the street, older ladies walking to church. The Mexican bakery a block from the park is busy, people coming out with white bags, and I remember the days when Timoteo has shown up early enough to get some sweet bread and coffee, already waiting for me.

But it's too early and we make only one round at the park before my feet start to hurt. There are men around, but not very many yet. I motion her to an empty bench.

You should put your purse in the shopping bag if it fits, I tell her.

It might, she says, about to try, but I put my hand on her arm.

Put this in your purse, I say, reaching into my bra and pulling out the little wad of bills and the piece of paper tucked between them. Quickly. And don't lose it.

You don't have to—

Quickly, I say again and she opens her purse and I drop the money inside, a deep pocket of nothing, just as I had suspected: No wallet, therefore no identification. No address book either, no gum, no mints, no tissues, no rolls of coins for the coffee machine, for the tampon dispenser, no nothing.

I left home when I was eighteen, I tell her. And somehow I made it here— I sigh just from how good it feels to tell someone who I am, how good it feels to admit to myself that I want her to know someone like me can help. But I know enough to let it rest, to not say the rest of the story. It's too long anyway, and we don't have all day.

All around us, the park starts to bustle with people. I know that most of us are waiting, but not everyone. Some are citizens, some are not. Some are out walking to their Sunday jobs, lucky to have something to do. Some are out walking just to relieve themselves of the boredom of being stuck at home, unemployed. To walk in the park, to sit in it as we are doing—it doesn't feel like a luxury, like I imagine for all those women on the television. They lounge on a beach and wish time would never end. Here, it ends the minute my man shows up.

And here he comes. I can spot Timoteo's small round shape even if his T-shirt is just as white and plain as everyone else's, and I raise my hand to capture his attention. But I don't wave it. I leave it straight up in the air like a flag.

Timoteo doesn't hug me or kiss me, but he grabs my hand and squeezes it briefly in greeting. He looks at Natalia for a moment, trying to decide if we're friendly or simply sharing space, and then I introduce her.

Natalia, I tell him. Mi amiga.

Timoteo nods at her and takes my hand again, impatient to get going. He asks her no questions, ready to move on with our lives. The day is early and I could invite Natalia to come with us to the Mexican bakery or to one of the food carts a few blocks away, where Timoteo likes to get a grilled corn cob sprinkled with chile and lime. But she has her life to live, and I have mine.

Bueno, I tell her. Suerte, and I say it with enough certainty and finality for her to know that she need do nothing—not return the shoes, not thank me for the money—except make the right choice when her man fails to show up in the park. I turn quickly before I have to see her eyes water from the fear of being all alone, and I clutch Timoteo's elbow when he turns around to look at her, a flash of what might be alarm on his face. Come, I tell him.

We walk back to the bus station and it's only when Timoteo sees that I'm having trouble walking that he spots the high heels. There's too many men in that park for you to be wearing shoes like that, he says.

His comment is neither stern nor kind: he knows my temperament well enough not to raise his voice to me. Even so, he's quiet for the few hours we wait in the bus station for our afternoon departure. He sits hunched over, elbows on his knees, as if he's contemplating Natalia more than me. He lets me have my silence. What we must look like to people, I wonder, neither one of us with a ring on our fingers.

Once we're on the bus, he takes the window seat, and it's only then that I see how exhausted he is. Nothing new is ever in his stories of how he got back—the coming back is always stressful, always tense—and his reliance on me to be there outweighs his doubt. If this is love, then it's as simple as it gets.

The bus driver comes down the aisle to do a final count and I lean back in my seat. I can hear him count under his breath and his slow, steady footsteps make me drowsy, remind me of old, stern Mrs. Rolnik back in Texas, pacing along the row of desks as she calmly read to us after lunch for fifteen minutes. Back then, I loved nothing more than the brown newsprint where I tallied numbers and blocked out letters, the cool feel of the desktop where I rested my head as she read. Back then there was so much hope. *Do something with your life, Griselda.* The rich feel of the ribbon in my hand when she placed it there, like a promise of things to come. The bus backs out of the station; nothing will stop its determination to take us back home. Ay, the cool feel of resting my head on the desktop.

Fifteen minutes. Just enough time to dream. Timoteo is already fast asleep, his head against the window, and I would do anything to rest my head against his shoulder, to nestle there. Ahead of me, the other women and their men face forward, together and stoic, all of them alert to the city streets, to what's passing by and what's coming. It's still love, the back of their heads seem to say to me. Not one woman is resting her head on her man's shoulder, so I sit upright and look straight out into the distance.

PRESUMIDO

They had it good, Juan and Daryl. Every now and then, Juan took on substitute teaching, and Daryl had steady work at the unemployment offices in downtown Fresno. Together, they made just enough to afford a small house on the edges of the Fig Garden district, where everyone around them was old and white. Daryl's parents, Claudette and Daryl Senior, had come over to the new house almost immediately. Not—Juan was surprised to learn—to inspect the house, but to encourage a housewarming, Daryl's mother sitting triumphantly in the kitchen and Daryl's pastor father much more reserved, his Sunday fire lit low.

Juan's father had paid a surprise visit on move-in day, too, but his stay was very short. He only stood in the doorways of the empty rooms, craning his neck in to see the stacked boxes, nodding slightly in approval, and Juan took his brevity as the quiet pride of acceptance. For all their disagreements, Juan had not disappointed his father like his brothers had, older than him and still living at home. Juan had built his own life: it was only Fresno and only a modest house and only Daryl, but it was another world entirely, a happy one.

41

Or so Juan thought sometimes, especially on that first day spent moving in the boxes, placing the furniture, filling up the space. Daryl took to the work with great excitement, fussy about where their belongings were stored and arranged, as if whatever was settled now would hold forever. The rooms refused to take shape, Daryl debating a table's position or pondering a color scheme, a back bedroom filled with unpacked boxes until they could look at paint samples on the weekend. "A very light blue," Daryl had said and Juan remembered his mother, Claudette, at the kitchen table, hands before her as if having a vision, those very same words leaving her mouth, Daryl Senior quiet beside her.

The task on that Wednesday had been, simply, to move into the house. For Juan, it wasn't about a very light blue or how far the couch was from the window. Nor was it about a housewarming party. It was about how the house should feel, with just the two of them in it. It was about whether or not this was their house or really just Daryl's.

His father had once said to Juan that he wished to live by himself, now that Juan's mother had left him, but he just couldn't say no to his sons. As Juan brought in more boxes, he thought of his father peering into the empty rooms, longing for a space of his very own, maybe. It had been, Juan realized, more than a few months since he had visited his father, but the move would tie up the rest of the week and the weekend was approaching.

On the weekends, they visited friends that Daryl had made—Bobby and Fred, Greg and Charlie, a wide circle of couples. All of the men seemed content, paired up and comfortable in the havens they had created for themselves and none showing any of the itch to run off to Los Angeles or San Francisco, never to return again. That was the feeling Juan got when he went along to these backyard barbecues. Something more than the impeccable green bushes was keeping out the rest of the world. Bobby and Fred lived on the north side of Fresno, which was noticeably becoming the rich side of town. Not just old and white, but rich. Their backyard had a pool; their friends sat around on expensive lawn furniture, plenty of seats for everyone. It was a long way from the poverty of scalped yellow grass and dirt driveways, the houses that both he and Daryl had grown up in. Some of the men at these gatherings may have been familiar with windows tilting in their frames from crumbling foundations, but they gave nothing away. Every weekend, it seemed more and more of them showed up. But once they revealed the small towns where they had once lived—Orange Cove, Cutler, Ivanhoe, Traver—Juan would never hear them speak of those places again.

That weekend, when Daryl and Juan arrived at the party, the news about their house spread. Bobby handed out white wine in real glasses. Someone had turned up the radio, a station with Evelyn "Champagne" King singing "Love Come Down," loud enough for dancing, but not enough to bother the neighbors. The chatter buzzed light and funny and the congratulations clearly pleased Daryl, who liked being the center of attention. He was a showy person, Juan knew, an only child. His mother doted on him, something Juan thought about when Daryl sought his affection. Bobby was asking about a housewarming party, but Juan held his tongue.

"Severina does a great job," he caught Bobby saying to Daryl. The plan was already in motion. She was the only woman Juan had ever seen at these parties, the one who prepared some of the food and brought it out in hot trays to the backyard, cheerful when the men complimented her cooking, but never lingering among them. She always went quickly back inside, and Juan, usually into a third or fourth drink by then, would sometimes glimpse her through the kitchen window.

The woman had caught him looking one time and stopped what she was doing for a moment. Her look of hard dissatisfaction dissolved when she had locked eyes with him and Juan had seized up at the way she had looked back, as if she might have been somebody he recognized, or who recognized him.

Juan would have called that shame, but it was more complicated than that, something closer to the old feelings he used to have when, out to movies with Daryl on their first dates, they had exited the the-ater and made their way back to the car. In those early days, it was easy to call it fear or threat, but if Juan had to be harsh with him-self, he felt those stares as judgment. He thought he was long past judgment.

A woman named Severina looking at him. Men from Kerman and Sanger and Terra Bella not speaking of those places anymore.

This was why the conversation about the new house and the party kept Juan silent and had him reaching for another glass of wine. He had wanted time to settle into the place, just him and Daryl, not even Daryl's mother in the kitchen to break the quiet, a differ-ent quiet than the complacency of Daryl's father. That quiet was not contentment. It was far from peace. He thought of how his parents had chosen their house years ago, if they had cared as much as Daryl did about split floor plans, how many bathrooms, not too many win-dows facing west. Juan studied the cheerful men in the backyard, so many of them smiling. They were men of the present moment, waiting for nothing. Everything they wanted, they already had. The music played and no one talked about work or trouble. Nothing out-side of the party mattered.

Juan had another wine. It wasn't the place to think about any-thing complicated.

"What do you think, Juan?" Daryl asked, but he hadn't been paying complete attention. Bobby and Daryl had been planning the party and the details had nothing to do with him, really.

"Sounds great," Juan muttered, but the words came out wrong, thin and dismissive, and he knew it as soon as he slurred them. So he placed his hand on Daryl's arm to show he was sincere about it.

He wandered off to visit with a group dipping their feet in the pool, as if to rehearse being a good host for Daryl's sake, so many men in the circle, he didn't have to listen to what any of them was saying.

For the rest of the party, he kept one eye on Daryl and the other on the kitchen window, waiting for a glimpse of Severina. But the kitchen stayed vacant and Daryl avoided eye contact long enough that Juan, with nothing to focus his attention, turned glum and distracted. Just as he finished another glass of wine, Daryl appeared by his side and whispered that they were leaving, that he had already said some goodbyes.

"They haven't even served the food," Juan protested, but Daryl led him by the elbow, a half embrace, his arm around his waist. It was a showy gesture, Juan knew, meant for the people who were watching them leave, and his instinct told him to push Daryl's arm away. Daryl held him firmly.

"You're drunk," he said in a very low voice, though there was no one to hear them, out past the side gate, past the kitchen door, out to the driveway where their car was parked. They had been among the first to arrive.

As Daryl pulled out of the driveway, in the fading light of sunset, Juan saw a figure emerge from the side gate, a short, squat silhouette that he knew was that woman, Severina, looking on as they edged the car into the street.

It embarrassed Juan to think what she had witnessed. On the way home, Daryl served him with a loaded silence, just as he always did when arguments spilled into the last moments of bedtime reading or television before Daryl turned out the light. Always, Daryl would say something into the dark and Juan wouldn't answer, the sting of Daryl's displeasure keeping him from sleep. This time, driving home across the central section of Fresno that was neither rich nor white, Daryl said, "If you're unhappy, you should just say so."

The words cut into Juan, but before he could think of anything to say in protest, the quiet in the car overtook him. Nothing came: not an answer, not a counteraccusation, not even an insult. When silence grew between them, it meant the argument was over. Daryl was especially good at finalities, just like his mother.

When they got home, Daryl busied himself in the kitchen, which was still in a state of being unpacked. He made a big show of it, noisy with each plate, the clatter of the utensils. Juan stayed in the living room and tried to ignore him, turning on the television and sinking into the couch, only to realize that neither of them had turned on the air conditioner when they'd gotten home. He didn't want to be the one to end the silence, though, by complaining. His stomach rumbled from the missed dinner and he could feel sweat start to bead on his forehead.

The television offered only the melodrama reserved for weekend afternoons: a woman in a hospital bed held a newborn baby and when the camera cut to another woman looking at her darkly, Juan knew the baby was in danger. He closed his eyes to the inevitable, impatient for the empty thrill of a story set up to carry itself out the way it was supposed to. This was the way the world worked. This was the way things were supposed to go. The baby would be rescued. Then the dark woman would come to justice. She would not be allowed to escape back into the world to wreck someone's happiness.

Such was the story, so he could close his eyes as it played out. The wine from the party tilted his head. He heard the sound of a woman plotting to herself in a voice-over. She was steadfast and determined, as if she didn't exist in a world where her plan would never work. Her words came sharp and mean, and the haze of the wine made Juan think it was really Severina speaking, her eyes stern through the window, exact in her stare, her silhouette in the driveway shaping into a startling, brilliant light.

"Juan?" Daryl shook him. "Wake up, baby."

He stirred to the dimmer light of evening, the local news flickering blue on the screen.

"You're sweating something awful," Daryl said, his hand on his forehead, gentle.

"It's hot in here," Juan mumbled.

"The AC is on." Daryl ran his hand through Juan's hair, damp with sweat. "You okay, papo?"

Daryl only spoke Spanish to him when he wanted to be sweet again.

"We missed dinner," Juan said. "I think that was it."

"We did," Daryl agreed, waiting for a moment, another bit of quiet between them. But this was a different quiet, one that had nothing to do with authority or deliberation. It was the quiet Juan had wanted. Something had settled and Juan knew not to add anything more.

"I can make dinner, papo," Daryl offered, but he didn't wait for Juan to answer. He went back to the kitchen and set about preparing them something to eat, this time with more restraint in the noise he made. A sort of calm came over the house that Juan recognized from growing up in a loud and contentious home. Whatever happened was over.

They ate dinner in front of the television, settling on a nature show from the public station, with long, quiet stretches of animals foraging in the snow, along a shoreline, in the branches of high trees. But the quiet suited Juan. Daryl, too, made no suggestion to change the channel. They left their plates on the coffee table. He placed his head on Daryl's shoulder because it was still throbbing from the wine. But Daryl, just by the way he caressed his head, must have taken this as an apology.

"We can have the party next weekend," Daryl said, kissing him on top of the head.

Juan thought of Daryl's father sitting in the kitchen, waiting patiently. Waiting for what, exactly, Juan wondered. On-screen, a bear swiped and swiped at salmon jumping upriver, his paws making no sound, just the rush of the water. A party next weekend, he thought to himself. Daryl had said it, so it would be.

They stayed like that for a while, Juan in Daryl's arms, until the nature show finally tuned out to the bubbly big band of *The Lawrence Welk Show*. The cheeriness was too much even for Daryl, who broke his hold to get up and change the channel.

Over the week, Daryl touched on the party plans, but never lingered on the subject. Saturdays were always for larger parties at Bobby and Fred's, Daryl said, as if thinking aloud, but Juan knew he was planning most of it without him. A happy hour, Daryl decided, on Friday, with maybe twenty people. It was summer and the schools didn't need substitute teachers; Juan knew that he would have to be the one to meet Severina that afternoon.

"She's coming at three thirty to set up," Daryl said.

On Friday, when Severina arrived, Juan answered the knock at the door to find her balancing two enormous foil pans precariously on each arm. "They're hot," she said, by way of hello, and rushed past him to the kitchen counter to set them down. She wiped her hands on her pants before she went back outside.

It was three thirty on the dot. Everything was going to happen just as Daryl wanted and there was nothing Juan could say about it.

Juan watched Severina in the driveway, unnerved by how she had brushed aside the formality of an introduction. He could picture Daryl on the phone talking to her, the two of them planning every last detail. Did she even know his name, Juan wondered. He thought about helping, but she moved with such assurance. They were Daryl's plans anyway.

She took out another tray from her car, an older Ford with bald tires and faded paint on the roof, along with a cardboard box. She tilted her chin at him and Juan stepped into the driveway, thinking she was asking for help. "No," she said, her eyes on the open door. "The flies."

The sweat cast dark circles in the armpits of her pink cotton T-shirt, a palm tree with the words PISMO BEACH stretched across her chest. The shirt, Juan thought, would have been unflattering on anyone, the cheap jersey already thinning at the shoulders. But once inside the house, before she did anything else, Severina drew an apron from the cardboard box and put it on, smoothing it down over the length of her body.

She glanced at the clock and turned on the oven to warm the food. "You have a very pretty house," she said.

"Thank you," he said. "I'm Juan."

"I know," she said. "Severina." She said it to him as if to remind him, as if he had forgotten. "Your friends will be here at five."

"Well, they get off work at five. And traffic . . ."

"If Bobby says five, they leave work early," she said. "I know your friends."

She unpacked the rest of the box: a vinyl tablecloth adorned with tropical fruits, paper plates and plastic glasses and utensils, a clutch of serving spoons. "Bobby said there would be twenty of you, but I made food for more." She walked to the door leading to the back-yard. "He didn't really say how big it was back here."

"Bobby hasn't been here," Juan said.

Severina turned to him for a moment, then looked again at the walls, taking in the house, as if she had expected everything to be in the same places as they were at Bobby and Fred's.

"I'm Juan," he said. "I'm Daryl's partner."

"You told me already," Severina said, smiling. "And Bobby is not." She opened the refrigerator and saw, with some disappointment, the six-packs still in their cartons. She took a few bottles out and grabbed the empty chest from the back steps. "Here," she said, handing him a beer and starting the quick work of dumping ice cubes from the freezer into the chest, arranging bottles. "Go ahead," Severina said, when he hesitated.

Severina's being weird

"Only if you have one," Juan said, but she continued with her work, glancing up at the clock.

"If I knew you better, maybe I would. But I'm working." She motioned for him to take the bottle, her hand still outstretched.

"You don't drink?" he asked.

"You're a very nervous man," she laughed, and placed the beer in his hand. "I'm not here to judge you."

"Have one with me," Juan insisted. He grabbed a beer from the chest and opened it for her.

Severina looked at the bottle and Juan felt as if his hand would start to shake if she didn't take it from him.

"You don't even have to drink all of it. Just to toast. To welcome you to our home."

"Salud," she said, taking the beer, clinking with him and swigging, to his surprise, a hearty pull from the bottle. In her rush to get things in order, she had kept the house in a bustle of noise, but it was quiet now, the oven ticking.

"So Daryl is your boyfriend," Severina said, less a question than confirmation.

"Yes, he is."

"How long have you been together?"

"Just a couple of years," Juan answered.

"Is this his house?"

"It's our house," he stammered. "We own it together."

"Very good," Severina said. She didn't take another drink from the bottle, nor did she put it down. "That's not very long to be together and own a house."

When she helped out at Bobby and Fred's, Juan knew, she was fastidious and rushed, cleaning up long before people even knew that she had gone. He knew that some people never really saw her, never even bothered to think of anyone in the kitchen, looking out at them, from the back windows, watching the couples. Juan knew that she saw much more than she let on.

"How long have you known Bobby?" he asked.

"Bobby and Fred," she said. "Both of them."

"Yes," he said. "Bobby and Fred."

"A long time. About five years. Ever since they've been together."

"So you know them well."

He thought of her watching some of the men at the party check each other out. Seeing, probably, the flirtations, the lingering looks when a back was turned. Severina knew them all very well.

"You get to know people when you feed them, yes," she said. She looked at the clock and put down the beer. "So the party is for Daryl," she said.

"It's a housewarming party. For both of us."

"Oh," she said. "I thought it was a birthday party."

"No," Juan said. "It's for both of us," he said again.

Severina laughed. "You're so nervous," she said. "My mother always said that if you say something twice, you don't really mean it."

He tried to laugh with her. "So I'm not really nervous? You said that twice."

"¿Verdad?" she said, with a familiarity that surprised him, the assumption that he spoke Spanish, that he should know how to speak it. He took another beer from the fridge.

"Forgive me for saying it, but Daryl is . . . do you speak good Spanish?" Severina didn't wait for him to answer. "Presumido. Do you know what I mean?"

Presumido. The word had weight, like the heat in the kitchen, with an added sting because Severina had to resort to Spanish to describe Daryl, the way he laughed with Bobby, with Fred, the way he wanted everyone to look at him

"No, I don't speak Spanish very well," Juan lied. The warm oven

He's afraid of judgement

was making the kitchen stuffy and, out in the backyard, the heat of the afternoon still bore down. He took a swig of beer and her eyes watched his hand with the bottle. He wondered if she had seen how much he drank at the parties.

"It means . . . uh . . ." She searched the air for the word. "I have a sister," Severina said, "who thinks a lot of herself. Nothing satisfies her. She's always looking somewhere else instead of right in front of her."

Juan knew what the word meant. Arrogant. Self-centered. So what was the word for Bobby? He took another swig of his beer. He could see that she had realized something.

"As my mom always used to say," Severina said, "te voy a decir una cosa pero no te vayas enojar . . ." but she stopped when Juan put his hand on his forehead, the heat of the oven getting to him, the beer too, and just when he thought she would continue with her unsolicited advice, the doorbell rang and she went to get it, the voices in the hallway greeting her in surprise and familiarity.

It was Greg, the ex–football player with the beefy arms, now a lawyer. It was Charlie, his equally handsome boyfriend with the slick-backed hair, slight and darkly handsome, with a career that Juan had asked about once but had long forgotten. When they walked into the kitchen, Severina handed them each a beer, but they hardly greeted Juan, Greg pointing one of his beefy hands at Severina's chest, at the palm tree on her pink blouse. "When did you go to Pismo Beach?" he asked cheerfully, Charlie looking on as if with great interest, and Juan took the moment to grab the ice chest and the vinyl table cover with the tropical fruit, as if there was still so much to do before the guests arrived.

Not long after, the buzz of conversation rippled from the kitchen windows, short bursts of loud laughter, and then big greetings when, apparently, Daryl arrived.

To Juan's surprise, the party stayed in the kitchen and the tight sliver of their new backyard looked immense in the emptiness and the glare of the late afternoon. They had no pool to cool them down, no tall bushes to block out the light. "My boyfriend took me once," he heard Severina say, to great laughter, though he didn't know what the joke was, what these men from Kingsburg and Lemoore and Fowler found so funny about Pismo Beach, about getting away, so far from here. Juan finished his beer and, before anyone came outside, he picked a final one from the ice chest.

How would he put it, if he had to? He had not wanted to host the party for the simple reason that he had not wanted to be under scrutiny. At the other barbecues, at the other parties, no matter who was around, Juan could take some refuge in not having to be the one on guard, the one who had to put on a good face for the rest of the group. He could be the quiet one looking into his own drink, lost in his own wandering mind, unsure of what to do about Bill, the one who had stopped him near the edge of the pool one night to tell him, very slyly, "I think we should hang out sometime."

He wondered if Severina had seen that, what she thought of that, if she judged him like he sometimes judged these men. He took a drink of beer, long this time, to make himself better about judging an already judgmental group, a petty group, all of them, the couples, the ones who lived on the north side of town, especially the ones who paused when he told them he was a substitute teacher, especially the ones who thought he wasn't good enough for Daryl, didn't deserve the peace of a new little house in the Fig Garden district, especially the ones who erased so much of where they came from, never speaking about it. And Daryl wanted to be like them, to put on airs in the same way that his mother did. They'd done this much together, but Juan knew that Daryl wouldn't be able to say that Juan wasn't enough.

Someone noticed him from the open back door and called out, "Juan!" He couldn't recognize the voice and so he didn't answer. He smoothed the vinyl covering on the table and realized he placed his hands down firmly to steady himself. "Juan!" he heard again, a different voice, and he looked up to see Greg, the beefy ex–football player, coming toward the table with one of the food trays. Charlie stepped out after him, a silver boom box in his grip, searching for an outlet along the wall. He was the one who liked the R&B station, searching the dials for a little while until he found his music, a song called "Forget Me Nots," the chorus coming in little jumps across the backyard, more and more of Daryl's friends wandering outside. Nowhere in the midst of them was a pink T-shirt and Juan eyed the back window to the kitchen, but the glare was too great. He saw little but the reflecting orange flash of the sun and he felt himself tilt his head as if to get a better view.

"You okay?" said Daryl. He had appeared beside him, as he always appeared beside him.

"I'm good," Juan said. "I need to eat."

"Just watch the drinking," Daryl said to him in a lowered voice. He turned his attention to the food at the table, preparing a plate that Juan thought was going to be for him but, instead, Daryl kept it in his own hand, lured into conversation by a new person Juan had never seen before, a guy who looked a bit like Greg, a bit like Charlie.

One person after another slipped out of their back door and Daryl lit up at the attention. Juan started another beer and ignored the food. There was nowhere to go until it was over. He looked for Bill, absently and with a flush of heat in his throat, trying to remember if Bill was even his name. He understood something about Daryl Senior, waiting in silence, a man who had not gotten out fast enough and now had nothing left but the little quiet he could carve out from the loud self-reverence of his wife, Claudette. He thought of his father, craning his head to look into their empty rooms, the burden of his brothers. Was that the same kind of frustration as Daryl Senior's? His mother was far away from his father now, in Corpus Christi.

To be alone was to be happy, he thought, but that didn't sound right—he didn't know if his mother was alone or not these days, or how his father wanted to be. Juan reached for another beer, surprised that his bottle was empty.

He drank and the heat reached his head, the back of his neck. It might be cooler inside, away from everyone for just a little bit, and he sidled his way along the strip of backyard, hands reaching out to touch him in greeting. Juan didn't know these people. He didn't know them like Severina knew them. In the kitchen, he planned to ask Severina what business she had telling him anything about Daryl and Bobby. Because what would she know, a woman who wore a shirt with PISMO BEACH across the front? Who knew if she had even been there, witnessed the place with her own eyes, if she knew anything about what it was like?

She didn't know what she was talking about. Or maybe he knew it already.

Severina was gone for the evening, the kitchen tidy again. She had been gone awhile, but Juan pretended that she had just left, that she had just missed being told off about minding her own business, lucky for her. If he concentrated hard, he could hear her beat-down car moving along the street very far away. Her car was the only sound in the world, the salmon jumping, the animals tracking across the hard-packed snow. She was going far away and she wouldn't witness how he was going to keep his distance from Daryl for the rest of the night. Juan could hear all the guests laughing, Daryl's loud voice above all of them. No other sound in the world. The heat was unbearable, even though the oven had long ago been turned off. Even the lights were out. The chair where Daryl's father had sat in silence was empty and Severina wouldn't witness that either, that question that Juan planned to ask him about being unhappy, about why he said nothing, about what he was waiting for. Sunset filtered in through the window. Juan looked out at the party, their compact backyard bringing everyone close. Good, solid friendships. A couple he didn't know nodded to each other as they explained something to another couple. He recognized none of them but they were wrong. They were wrong about whatever they were talking about, whatever they were hoping for. Wrong, wrong, wrong. Juan wiped at his forehead, brought his hand down to his throat. If he wanted another beer, he would have to go back outside, so he sat in the empty kitchen chair to gather himself, just a few minutes, because it would be hard to be surrounded by so much wrong without, finally, having to say something about it.

SUSTO

No one in town even knew the old man's name, but they pretended they did after he was found dead by the foreman one day at the end of winter. The foreman, as he told it later that morning to the others at the Royal Dutch Bakery during their coffee break, had stopped the tractor midrow when he couldn't make out the strange silhouette deep in the vines. The grape farmer had sent him out at dawn to begin the spring prep on the vineyards and he had spotted something in the distance. The foreman shut off the tractor, spooked by the dark form lying in the row. Whatever it was, it was too big to be a dead coyote, a rabid stray dog that had collapsed on its way to hiding out before dying, as sick animals sometimes do. The dark form didn't move. The quiet of dawn only deepened the eeriness.

The foreman didn't tell the men at the bakery that he had stayed on the tractor and waited for the sun to break into its truest light before he dismounted. As he got closer to the shadow, he could tell that it was a person, a man by the look of the clothes: a white T-shirt yellowed in the armpits, pants that may have been part of a good suit too many years ago, and leather shoes worn and woeful at the soles.

That's all the foreman saw of him—the clothes had been all he had
to confirm that the body was indeed a man, because the body's head
was buried in the dirt. Like a goddamn ostrich, the foreman told the
others gathered around the Formica tabletop listening to him.

He hadn't meant to spit the words out like that, just as the young
waitress came around with the coffeepot. The other men had fallen
silent at both his story and the conviction that the waitress shouldn't
be overhearing terrible things. She served their coffee and looked at
none of them, but she caught the foreman's eyes just as she finished
her pouring, and she seemed to search his face for the source of his
contempt.

Did she know the man? he wanted to ask her, since she was a
Mexican girl whose family let her work on Sundays, and the man
whose head had been lifted from the dirt was as brown as she was.
He might have guessed from the brown of the man's hands if he had
been brave enough to look, but it had taken the weekend deputy,
pulling the man's head from the ground like a dandelion weed and
brushing away the caked dirt from the eyelids, to confirm that the
dead man was an older Mexican.

But the foreman didn't ask the Mexican girl anything and she
walked back behind the counter as if she hadn't heard a word. The
other men took over the story. They knew the weekend deputies
and who would have been on the Sunday shift and that the man was
probably some drunk who wound up so far out in the fields and that
it was probably Dennis, the youngest of the Kenmore brothers, who
had shown up from the sheriff's office. The foreman let them talk.
He said nothing about how long he had sat on top of the tractor before he felt safe enough to go back to the farmhouse and summon
help. He kept quiet about needing the sun to come up to chase away
the darker suspicions that this was the devil's work and to help him
see it all in the cold logic of a robbery gone wrong. He didn't say that
he had waited for Dennis Kenmore at the side of the road, the trac-

tor idle in the middle of the field, and the shape of the man with his head buried in the dirt so still in the distance that he swore at one point it moved.

One of the men remembered, a couple of years back, a teenage boy who had been found in one of the town alleyways, a dropout from the high school who dealt measly amounts of weed but had nonetheless been knifed for whatever he'd been carrying. The boy had been as thin as his empty wallet, the man said, on account of all the harder drugs he did, but he was proof that even a few dollars was more than enough reason for someone to do such a thing.

people are ruthless

The Zacarías kid, confirmed another. The oldest one in that bunch, too. His mother raised him better than that.

It's one thing to be looking for trouble at that age, said another. But an old man? Probably buried his head himself out of shame for whatever he'd been up to.

Who said he was old? The quietest man finally spoke. Who said he had anything to be ashamed about?

Well, he wasn't a teenager. And what's an old man doing out in the middle of a field if he ain't working?

The other men turned to the foreman. Did he work for you?

I've never seen him in my life, the foreman answered. But he didn't tell them that he had barely been able to look at the man. Dennis Kenmore held him up by the scruff and roughly brushed away the dirt from his eyes. The eyes must have been shut and yet he wasn't sure.

He would've recognized him if it had been a worker. He would've told us the name.

Like I said, I've never seen him in my life, the foreman repeated.

Last night was Saturday and it's the beginning of the month so people have money in their pockets. Poor guy probably got drunk at John Henry's and went off with some new people and they robbed him and dumped him in the fields. That's what happened.

An ostrich? someone asked.

The foreman didn't answer. He didn't want to say the words again. The waitress behind the counter slid a tray of bread into one of the cases, as if she hadn't heard them talking.

If he's a good Christian, someone will miss him in church, the quietest man said, though it was Sunday and not a single one of them had been to a service in years.

For the rest of the morning, the foreman's discovery left him at a strange crossroads of somberness and dread. The other men had exited the bakery by noon, but the foreman sat alone, reluctant to return home. Some churchgoers stopped by after services and he watched them select bread from the cases for their evening meals. They were older people overdressed for the cold in the Valley, still wrapped in scarves as they waited, their gloved hands clutching dollar bills. With their backs turned to him, the foreman couldn't tell if they had come from the Catholic service on the far side of town or from the Presbyterian church with the manicured lawns and high green shrubs. They were dutiful no matter who they were, waiting patiently for the waitress to serve them, saying hardly anything beyond their pointing fingers and maybe a thank-you he could barely hear. His coffee cup had gone cold but he hadn't bothered to raise his hand for a refill. The foreman listened to the older churchgoers shuffle across the floor, tap on the glass cases for the better bread, rustle their paper bags tight against the cold before they went back outside. What little he could catch of their faces when they passed by betrayed nothing of what they might have heard in church that day. He found himself surprised that he wondered about it at all, watching them, his mind on how another Sunday morning had silenced on by. Had they heard that it was not wise to love this world or anything in it? What would that mean, he wondered, if they knew a man had been found dead in the fields?

What else was there but the fields and the orchards?

The bakery had emptied and was suddenly quiet. The waitress stepped away from the register and wiped down the front counters. She began to slide trays of unsold bread out of the cases and took them one by one to the back of the bakery, not looking at the foreman. The longer the silence went on between them, the more he knew he wasn't to ask for another refill of the coffee. Though he knew the bakery wouldn't close until three, the foreman waited until she stepped into the back of the shop, then rose and stepped into the day, the bells on the front door jingling behind him. He imagined she was relieved by the sound of his leaving and he felt freed in a way as well. He didn't want to think about that man, or look at a face that knew what he was thinking. The foreman took in the empty street, looked this way and that, but no one was about. Everyone had retreated to their own homes and he had no choice, he knew, but to return to his, a small house he rented on the edge of town, close enough to the county road to see the cars coming and going from bigger places in the Valley. He walked up the street to a corner market, its windows already starting to glow against the meager light of the winter day, and he bought a bottle of whiskey from the bored-looking clerk who, for a moment, looked at him as if he had had a sudden and burning question, only to give him his change without a word.

The foreman got back to his small house by three in the afternoon. He took his whiskey to the front porch and unscrewed the cap on the bottle. The daylight had gone milky and the Sierras over in the distance had already steeled themselves purple. He would drink, the foreman thought, until he could no longer give himself over to the chill of the winter trees sinking into the dark. He would watch the endless parallel rows of the fields blend their green edges beyond discernment, no moon rising. He would track the first few wisps of the winter fog forming almost as soon as the sun slipped down. By then the day would be over and he could forget about the terrible way in which it had begun.

The whiskey was warming him. The bare branches of the fruit trees, which had let in the afternoon's craggy light, closed in. The fog deepened, coming in low to about the height of the vineyards. Far off in the distance, the red taillights of cars heading to bigger towns reminded him of the woman who had been in his life many years ago, just long enough to begin talk of marriage, but not long enough for doubt to break its hold on his heart. Frustrated with him, she left to Los Angeles and the foreman never heard from her again. Why does he remember now? His eyes followed the red taillights getting smaller and smaller in the distance. He expected them to disappear, but they steadied after a moment, two pinpoints of red light in the winter dusk. He traced the lights moving along the road, then followed them as they froze, seemed to change direction, coming now toward the farmhouse. The foreman blinked his eyes to be sure, losing the lights in the fog momentarily before making them out again. The red lights traveled too slowly to be a car, he thought, and they floated along what he was sure was one of the outer vineyards. The foreman stood up to get a full view. He squinted against the dark and the fog, against the whiskey, aware of the anonymity of his small house, of the enormity of the dark world.

The lights weren't so far off now. He could make out the edge of the vineyard where the red pinpoints finally emerged from the leaves and fixed on him like a set of eyes. No, they *were* a set of eyes, his sight adjusting to the darkness of the field, and now he could make out the vague outline of a man's body, the glow of a white shirt, still and unmoving. He could make out the slumped posture of an older man. The foreman sensed a stern grip deep in his chest, seizing him to complete attention, but it was not alarm or terror, but rather something like pity. He knew who it was.

What do you want? the foreman finally called out, but nothing came.

What do you want from me? he tried.

The figure did not move. Nor did it make a sound. The foreman kept waiting for something to break, to hear soft footfalls in the dirt, or the vines snapping off to let pass whatever needed to return to the darkness of the field. He tensed in anticipation, but nothing broke, and he felt his body give way to a lightness, like stepping off the last bit of solid ground and into a deep, calm pool of water. He was still on the porch—he could sense the wooden slats beneath his boots and the wintry air pinching at his skin—but he trusted the buoyancy of the voice he knew he was about to hear, and he closed his eyes, hoping to understand what it had to say. The voice was on the brink. He could feel it about to come out of his own mouth, an involuntary, flattened whisper, a last word in a dream. The foreman felt himself floating, first to the edge of the porch, and then somehow retreating into the darkness of his house. Out there, at the edge of the vineyard, the foreman caught the flicker of the old man before he returned to the fog. The night collapsed around him and when he opened his eyes, he heard the call of the rooster greeting dawn at one of the farmhouses somewhere across the fields. He was in his bed, his clothes still on, and at his side, the letter that had been returned to him from somewhere in Los Angeles. He did not remember opening it. *I miss talking to you, though I know it is hard for both of us.* The light in the hallway had been left on, trying to brighten the house. *I keep hoping you still want to hear from me.*

He rose and put the letter in the back of the top dresser drawer. He had work to do—there was always work to do in the fields—and he walked out to his truck, his head still buzzy from the night's drinking. Not all of the men from the usual Sunday gathering would be there. Some still worked, but the retired ones and the ones without wives drank coffee there daily. He had gotten into bed somehow without eating dinner and he convinced himself that he was going to the bakery because he was hungry. His stomach growled in agreement, but the bakery served no breakfast. That would be at the P&A diner around the corner, but he knew no one there. If he peered through the diner's plate-glass window, he would recognize no one, and no one would turn to look at him, as did the three of the Sunday men now, spotting his truck in surprise.

You look like hell, said one of them, and waved the waitress over. Bring him a sweet roll, something with a little sugar in it.

Sit, said another, and when the foreman did so, they all waited until the waitress poured him a cup of coffee and placed the pastry in front of him.

Lots of things can drive a man to drink, said the third man. Ain't no shame in it.

Who says I've been drinking?

They scoffed at him. Come on now, said the eldest one, the one who had been retired the longest and knew how to temper a conversation. Maybe not this morning, but you sure look like you were up to something last night.

The foreman took a drink of the coffee and it roiled his stomach in bitter. I got bothered by what I saw.

Has the Kenmore boy been out to see you?

About what?

About finding out more on who that man was.

I talked to him yesterday when he came out to the vineyard, said the foreman. He wrote some things in his little deputy's notebook and that was it.

The elder, the one who had lost his wife to cancer over five years ago, the one who never touched a drop because she had been a devout Baptist, who had never set foot in the liquor store even after he buried her, rapped his knuckles gently on the Formica tabletop. Mark my words, he said. Kenmore raised some smart boys, but you're going to be waiting a long time to hear anything about an old Mexican found in the fields.

Sounds like you're telling him to hit the bottle again tonight, said one of the men.

That's not what I'm saying.

If Kenmore's not going to come around to ask him anything . . .

Is that why you were drinking? the elder asked. You worrying yourself over a man you're never going to know? That no one is ever going to know?

suspicious

The foreman couldn't bring himself to say what he had seen in the vineyard when dusk had arrived. They wouldn't believe him if he tried to describe the sensation that had overcome him, the feeling of words literally in his mouth, as if he had it in him to say something without thinking.

Drink if you want to, said the elder. I'm telling you to stay sober because Kenmore will want to talk to you again. You don't want people in town talking about how you turned into a big drunk just because you found a body out in the fields. This is a terrible world but people have held it together over more than you'll ever see.

invalidating his feelings

One of the other men rose to his feet, sensing a lecture about to come on. He left extra dollar bills and slid them over to the foreman, just enough for the coffee and the sweet roll. You drink as much as you want, he whispered conspiratorially to the foreman. Whatever you need to forget.

Nobody needs to forget, said the elder. If you all went to church on Sundays, you'd know what I was trying to say.

With all due respect, said the third man, rising to join his friend, you don't go to church either and reading a Bible at the kitchen table doesn't count for much. He patted the foreman on the shoulder. I can't do a sermon on a Monday morning. But you take care of yourself.

The two men exited and the foreman was left with the elder, the waitress standing at the register, wiping nothing down. The sweet roll sat uneaten and it occurred to the foreman that he had no idea

how the bakery did on weekday mornings, with the churchgoers nowhere to be found.

I grew up in a small town in Arkansas, said the elder man after
a time. My wife grew up about five miles from where I lived. Towns
spaced out like they are here in the Valley, couple miles in between,
fields all around. She came with me out here when her parents died
in a car accident and she had no people anymore. That's what people
did in those days. They went out to California. We raised a family
out here, a boy and a girl. My boy died on the young side. Doing
foolish things. But our daughter moved on out to the coast and had
our grandkids before my wife passed.

I know it's been a while, said the foreman, but people still remember her.

That's my point, said the elder. You remember her. People knew
her. I started coming to the bakery in my fifties, when my wife told me
she thought I was spending too much time alone. She said it was good
to get out and go have a conversation with people. Remind everybody
that you're still around. You see what I'm trying to tell you?

The foreman looked blankly at him. I'm sorry, but I don't.

Do you think for a minute if I'd gone missing that people
wouldn't notice? You're telling me you wouldn't worry just a little bit
if I hadn't shown up on Sunday morning to drink coffee? I come here
rain or shine.

You do, the foreman agreed.

This is a small town, the elder said. And you don't think it says
something that no one knew that man? That you didn't know that
man?

They sat for a while without the foreman answering him and the
moment for pondering slipped right on past into a silence that felt
like truth.

I'll tell you what, said the elder, it's hell on earth when you have
to sit with the fact that nobody will miss you. That's what's tearing

you up about that old man. Terrible thing to die lonely, without anybody knowing you passed.

The elder sighed and rose with great difficulty from the table. I have to get the day started, he said. He stared at the bills on the table. Will that cover it? he said, turning to the waitress.

It will, she said, though she was at the counter.

The elder took a long time walking out and after the door jingled shut, the waitress walked over to pour the foreman another coffee. Don't worry about the check, she said. He can pay me the rest tomorrow morning.

I'm sorry, he said, patting for his wallet. I left the house . . .

You look terrible, she said. You look ill.

I didn't sleep well last night.

Susto, she said. You know Spanish? You know what that is?

I've heard the word, but I don't know what it means.

She searched upward to find the right meaning. A scare, she tried. But in your soul, deep down.

Susto, the foreman repeated, and he wondered for a moment if he should tell her what he had seen and felt. He worried that she, too, wouldn't believe him, and then he worried that she would.

I just want to say, said the waitress, that Mr. Whittaker is very mistaken. We know who the old man in the field was.

We?

The neighborhood, she said. Our neighborhood. It was Don Facundo. He was the old man who lived at the last house at the end of the street, so everyone saw him coming and going. Facundo Nieves was his name.

Facundo Nieves . . . I've never heard of him.

He worked with the cattle farmers, not out picking the fields, so you wouldn't know him, she said. But we knew him.

Someone came through the door. The foreman heard the bells jingle and he could tell from the deliberate footsteps that it was an older person. The waitress went back behind the counter. A woman's voice, phlegmy and strained, asked for a loaf of bread and the fore-man, with his back turned, could make out the faint clink of coins. She had bought the day-old Sunday bread. Gracias, Doña Lena, he heard the waitress say, a voice full of familiarity and knowing, and he heard the slow footsteps walk out, the bakery quiet again.

The waitress came back to his table. She sat down in the spot where the elder had been, the chair in a bit of sunlight, and he caught, for the first time, the name on her tag. Margarita.

Don Facundo rented out the house at the end of our street and had lived there for over twenty years. He had a wife and three chil-dren, but she wanted to go back to Durango. One day, she went to Mexico with the kids and never came back. He's been living alone ever since. But we kept our eye on him. We knew he was there.

Did you tell the Kenmore boy?

He hasn't come around to ask as far as I know. He doesn't know where to look. But you should tell him, she said, rising from the table. He'll listen to you.

Say his name one more time? the foreman asked.

Facundo, she said. Facundo Nieves. Nieves is snow, a funny name for a man from Durango, as he always said. But it snows in Mexico too. She reached for the untouched sweet roll. You should go to the P&A and eat something.

Thank you, he said. I think I will. Margarita waved to him as he walked out of the bakery and back onto the street that looked every bit as empty as it did on Sunday afternoon. The sun was bright. He drove up the street, wondering if Margarita knew anyone at the P&A, if she would ask after a man who had come in for breakfast and sat alone, a man whom the waitresses at the P&A wouldn't rec-ognize. He drove past the large plate-glass windows but didn't stop. He drove past the liquor store, where the bored-looking clerk stood at the counter as he always did, oblivious to the fact that the foreman had thought for a moment about getting another bottle of whiskey. But there was work to do, empty stomach or no, and so he drove on out to the small house he rented on the edge of town and got to it.

He had trellis work, checking the posts and the wires for breaks before the workers came out to strip and prune the vines to prepare for spring. He walked out into the vineyard, the day bright and almost warm, the sun good on his hands. When he had to step under the vines to test a wire, he could feel the cold of the soil seep through to his feet. He went deeper into the vineyard, the work going quickly, even though he was hungry. The foreman turned every now and then and could see his small house in the distance, the air clear, and the sky open. When he bent down to inspect a post sagging at the anchor, his head rushed, and he had to steady himself before continuing. The days of working on an empty stomach were long over. It would have to be a short day. The sky held even bluer, even brighter. A bit of sweat broke on his brow and he swiped it away. He would have to break soon and head back to the house to eat. But it felt good to work, to not think about the old man who had a name now. Facundo, the foreman said aloud, out in the vineyard where no one could hear him. Facundo Nieves, he sighed, and held his sweaty face up to the blue sky, a small part of him hoping that a miraculous snow would come out of nowhere and alter the world, soothe him from what he had seen.

He was in the middle of the field, the house a little dot in the distance. Over there, the sound of the cars traveling along the county road, and he could see them, clear as anything. The few leaves that hadn't fallen from the vines fluttered in a light, cool breeze. Over by the house, some movement caught his eye, and he knew it was Kenmore's son coming out to speak to him. The foreman started walking back, bristling at the inefficiency of having to stop in the middle of a row. He compensated by double-checking his work as he started back toward the house. In the distance, at the end of the row, he could make out the silhouette of Kenmore waiting for him, but he kept his eyes on the vines, the posts, the wires, the leaves. He worked his way back until he got close enough to see that the silhouette was not Kenmore's son.

The foreman caught the whiteness of the shirt first and stopped. How could it be, out in the brightness of the day? He took one cautious step forward, but he knew what he would confirm if he moved any closer. He stood in the vineyard and looked this way and that, but he could see no one else and no one, he knew, could see him. The sky was so vast, accepting all the light. His loneliness struck him like a rattler lurking in the vines, swift and vicious, a small and hidden thing that he bypassed daily, unaware. The bewilderment came again, his chest beginning to collapse, and he thought of the letter and the lines he'd written, unanswered. *I've been with you. I'll be with you. I want to be with you.* He felt himself break into understanding, that he could beg forgiveness from Facundo Nieves for not having known him, some mercy to match his longing. He felt, instead, a bubbling directive. He opened his mouth as if to say something he had known all along. To his surprise, the feeling came in Spanish. He collapsed to his knees and anticipated all the things that had to be said, but only a single word came in his own tongue. *Dig*, it said, and under the bright blue winter sky, the foreman felt his hands push into the dirt. What do you want? he heard himself ask, though he could not stop himself. *Dig*, he heard again, from inside, and his fingers moved past the thin topsoil and into the colder, rockier layers underneath.

THE REASON IS BECAUSE

Never mind that except for Shawna, the daughter of one of the elementary school librarians, no other girl in Nela's junior class had ever gotten pregnant. The way her mother made it sound, girls her age were pushing strollers around United Market, standing in line with their WIC coupons instead of being in school. But Nela knew this wasn't true. The looks she got at the grocery store proved it. Shawna, a skinny white girl who had worn long sweaters to her knees to fool everyone, had been sent off to relatives in San Diego long before she had her baby. Nela had nowhere but here and she was the only one.

The only what? The only pregnant girl in school? The only young mother? "The only girl your age . . ." as her mother would say when she started in on her. From the moment Nela had to admit to her mother what had happened because of Lando Quintanilla, she had felt the word *only*, understood why Shawna had gone away to San Diego, where she could be only without anybody knowing her.

Nela had dropped out of classes before she had begun to show and didn't miss school at first. Not the gossip and the whispering, which her friend Luz reported to her. But it was September again and the baby was waking at dawn, with the worst of the summer heat giving way to cooler mornings. Nela took to sitting at the top of the stairway leading up to their second-floor apartment. She held the baby and longed for the boring days at the high school. At least there, her daydreaming didn't seem so pointless. She looked down at the parking lot of the Las Palmas complex and watched it empty out by eight thirty in the morning. Nela's mother scoffed with resentment, muttering about their neighbors making too much money to be on Section 8. This wasn't true, Nela knew, judging by the cars coming back coated with the fine dust of the fields. People were finding jobs that might pay under the table to keep an apartment like theirs from scrutiny. It was a savvy that Nela understood now, with the baby in her arms, and it made her sad for knowing it, for having grown into wishing for something different.

From what Luz had told her, Lando Quintanilla was still walking around the hallways at school like he had gotten away with something, like everyone didn't know that he was the father of Nela's baby. Lando, who used to leave school at the end of every day without even a pencil in his hand, was in it for real now, according to Luz. Come next June, he of all people would have a diploma.

What he would do with it was another matter but, as Nela's mother kept insisting, he recognized now that it was important to graduate. "His elevator don't go all the way to the top," her mother said, "but at least he'll go places." Whatever places those were, Nela's mother hadn't been, and neither had her father, wherever he was. By the emptiest part of her morning, the parking lot was nearly deserted. Nela could hear the faint but constant filter of TV game shows through the open windows. By noon, everyone could hear the stuttering rush—"¡Córrele, córrele!"—that sent Doña Hortencia, who played bingo on Radio Bilingüe, running to the pay phone in the laundry room, too late to call in her prize.

Always too late, Nela thought, every time she saw her, but it was hard not to think of herself at school, pushing away the books that had been placed in front of her. She knew now that a boy was nothing to wish for and that even a dumb wish like Doña Hortencia's bingo playing was better than what she had ended up with. The look of dejected pride that Doña Hortencia wore on the way back from the laundry room depressed Nela. "Bien safada," Nela's mother said of her, but Nela always smiled back at Doña Hortencia. The other women at Las Palmas left the door to the common laundry open, even when the manager complained. They maintained a small stack of dimes on top of the phone, just in case Doña Hortencia got there in time but had no coins. Nela envied her a little. At least she was still dreaming.

A little help was all Doña Hortencia needed, a voice always calling from the dark doorway of her apartment, encouraging her to run, run, run. Nela could only wish for as much, passing the days mostly on the steps, sometimes with the baby, sometimes not. Her mother turned on the television in the morning and kept it on all day. Whenever the baby woke for a feeding, Nela ate too, a single piece of bread folded over with something in the middle. By three in the afternoon, when the Donahue show came on, Luz would stop by to report on school.

"He's still there," Luz always told her, as if nothing was going to change. Nela secretly wanted Lando to drop out, if only so her mother would move on to someone else's failure. Today, Luz said it even before she made her way up the stairs to join her. She put down her math book with a cover made from a United Market paper bag, her otherwise pristine Pee-Chee folders with nothing in them. She spent the days with her chin in her hand, writing the name of the boy she swooned over in tiny letters. ALONSO ALONSO ALONSO, as if she could will him into her life.

Luz was no fool. She went to school in the long denim skirts that her parents ordered her to wear, her hair plain and straight all the way down the back. But she saw Alonso on the sly whenever she could. Luz said, almost casually, "The Raisin Day Festival is this weekend."

Nela had almost forgotten about their town's annual parade. "Are you going?" Nela asked.

"Just to the carnival. It starts tonight. You want to come?"

"My mother won't want to babysit."

"So bring the baby with you."

"She would never let me take the baby out in the middle of all those people."

"Whose baby is it?" Luz asked. "Hers or yours?"

It was tough talk from Luz, arrogant and full of her not know-ing the long drag of Nela's mornings, the hours spent as she second-guessed herself. It made Nela think of the days after the baby was born, agreeing to name the baby after Lando. The last name, right down to the Junior and everything. "It's not that easy, Luz," Nela said.

"Sure it is." Luz pointed down the stairs and Nela followed her finger out to the horizon beyond the parking lot. "One step at a time." Luz marched down a few of them as if to show her but turned back quickly when she saw that Nela was unmoved. "Seriously, though. Or get Lando to care of it. He doesn't even give you alimony."

"Child support, mensa. We never got married."

The baby stirred a bit but Luz, still looking like she might have an answer to that, stayed quiet for a moment.

"You know what I mean," she said, her voice a little lower once she was sure that the baby had gone back to sleeping. "He doesn't help you. Does he even come over?"

"Sometimes," Nela answered. The real answer was almost never. His visits came unannounced, a friend of his waiting down in the parking lot with the car still running while Lando ran up the stairs to knock on their door. Sooner or later, their neighbors would look out to see who the car belonged to, Lando's friend tossing a half-lit cigarette to the cement when the staring got to be too much. A quick honk told Lando to hurry up. "At least the baby sees him," Nela's mother would tell her. "It's important for a baby to see his father."

Nela's mother said stupid things like that, blind to the real reason Lando came around. He was checking on Nela, making sure that no other guy was around, the way he stood in the doorway, barely holding the baby and crooking his neck to see past Nela into the apartment. It angered Nela that he would want no one in her life, even when he didn't want to be with her. She knew better now, just as she knew better that it had been a mistake to name the baby as she had, just as she knew better why her mother hadn't kicked her out of the apartment when she announced her pregnancy. "You're her dependent," Luz had explained, one of the few times she used a big word right. "They'd move her downstairs to the efficiency apartments, and no one wants one of those."

"Maybe I'll go to the parade tomorrow morning," Nela said.

"The parade's boring," said Luz. "If I want to see a bunch of kids on the back of a truck, I'll go to my tío's house. Come to carnival."

"The baby—"

"Leave the baby here," said Luz. "Or take him with you." She sighed heavily and tilted her head at Nela, impatient. "See—you just don't know how to make people do what you want."

"What do you mean?"

"All you have to do is listen to what your mom wants you to do and then do the other thing," said Luz. Before Nela could protest that Luz was wearing the long denim skirt and pressed white blouse that her parents demanded, she saw how Luz had only given in on the clothes to gain their trust. If she followed orders, she could go places. She could go to the carnival. She could see Alonso on the sly.

"Your problem is you ask," Luz continued. "You don't have to ask anybody if you don't want to. No matter what you do, it's always the right thing. Because you want to do it. See what I mean?"

If Nela had been in the mood for an argument, she would've told Luz that she was the one who had encouraged her to keep staring back at Lando Quintanilla. But the baby wasn't Luz's fault or Lando's or hers, Nela told herself. That was her mother's way of thinking. The baby was just a baby, and she could put it to bed while she went to the carnival, just for a little bit.

Nela stood up, the baby still quiet in her arms, and left Luz waiting at the bottom of the stairs. She gently opened the door of the apartment and passed inside, her mother looking up to see if the baby was sleeping or not. Nela left the door slightly ajar to signal Luz to wait for her, that she wouldn't be long. Before her mother could whisper, "What's Luz still doing here?" Nela had put the baby down in its crib.

"I'm going to the carnival real quick," she told her mother, and rushed to the door before her mother could protest. "Where do you thinking you're going?" her mother hissed after her from the landing, but Nela didn't answer, Luz following in surprise right behind.

"That's how you do it," Luz said, her voice catching with nerves, since she wasn't the one doing the brave thing. But that's how it was, Nela decided. Everyone knew better than she did, everyone knew what had to be done. She took no comfort in Luz's encouragement as they headed for the park in the center of town. It was as hard to keep walking as it was to not turn back.

Later on, when she returned to the apartment, she would endure her mother. But right now, the walk in the fading afternoon light reminded Nela that it was Friday and she could see the weekend anticipation on the faces passing by as cars drove over to the carnival. She was aware of their ages now, the young married couples, the ones without children, none of them tired from being up at six in the morning because of a baby. Girls their age were heading to the park on foot, little brothers and sister in tow. This was the crowd they would get—the babysitters, the ones who took the children out to leave the homes with a temporary peace. This was the order of things in their town, and Nela thought of her mother back at the apartment, the things she must be saying under her breath.

The carnival was still a day away from being full tilt, but the kiddie rides were running and so were more than a few food and game booths. Enough people milled around to make it hard to find a seat, but they caught an empty spot at one of the wooden picnic tables. Nela had left the apartment too quickly to bring money along. Luz, looking around for any sign of Alonso, made no motion to buy her even a soda for the trouble.

"There he is," Luz said, but Nela had spotted him long before that, Alonso tall and shallow-chested, still wearing the pressed dress shirt that his churchgoing parents bought for school. He wore them even on Fridays, when all the school athletes, not just the football players, were asked to wear their letterman jackets. Alonso was on the track team, slightly hunched, his strides long and gangly. Nela had never found him attractive, but now that she was away from school, away from Lando Quintanilla, away from all the boys at the high school, she had had a long time to consider what was desirable and good. Like Luz, Alonso was practicing a careful rebellion. Like Luz, he was biding his time until he was out of his parents' grasp. She respected this patience now, all the hatching of their secret plans.

"He brought a friend," Nela said.

"That's his cousin," Luz said quickly. Nela thought her answer was too forced, too nonchalant. She kept her eye on the cousin as the boys approached and, the closer they got, the more assured Alonso appeared by comparison. His cousin stood beside him, smaller and rounder.

"This is my cousin Javi," Alonso said.

"Hi, Nela," Javi said, and as soon as he said her name, Nela knew that Alonso and Luz would be leaving them alone.

Alonso took solid hold of Luz and started to pull her into the crowd with his long, awkward arms. "You want something to eat?" Luz asked her, as if they were coming back soon. "I'll bring you something, promise," she said, calling over her shoulder.

"I can get you a soda," Javi offered. "I'm kind of thirsty anyway." He dug into his pockets and pulled out a couple of dollar bills.

"That's nice of you," Nela agreed, afraid to disappoint him. Javi ducked over to one of the concession carts to stand in line and she watched him, squat and dumpy, how ridiculous to send him along at all, a guard by Alonso's family against whatever trouble they thought their goody-goody son could get into. It was too early out, the park too full of little kids, for anyone to carry on like that. Nela felt a little sorry for Javi, his fat head waiting patiently for the concession line to move forward, oblivious to what other teenagers did when they had a chance to be alone. His concentration was on the food order, his pudgy fingers counting two of each thing to the man in the paper hat. It was impossible to think of him as the same age as Alonso, as Luz, as her. He looked like one of the freshmen boys trapped in an adolescence that wouldn't hurry along, couldn't turn him fast enough into a guy like Lando Quintanilla, who filled out a plain white T-shirt, his dark biceps taut just from resting his arms on the desk, a senior who did things in his tío's Buick Riviera that a boy like Javi could only imagine.

He came back to the table with his arms so loaded with food and an eagerness to eat that Nela was hesitant to ask if any of it might be for her. Javi pushed a small plate of nachos and a soda her way.

"I don't have any money on me," she said.

"That's okay," he said, with a mouthful of taco.

"You go to school here?"

"I'm from Reedley," he said. "Not here."

"What year are you?"

"Same age as Alonso. I'm a senior."

"I wouldn't have guessed that."

"Believe it," said Javi. They ate for a little while before Javi said, "We met before. Only, I think you don't remember. We met here at the carnival. Three years ago or something."

Javi was right. Nela didn't remember. She remembered meeting a cousin of Alonso's but if Javi was short and pudgy now, she couldn't imagine the weak impression he would have given her back then. She had been full of easy distraction then, the playfulness of being with friends her age at the park for the first time without their parents, the older boys showering them with attention. She and Luz had gotten whistles all night. By the time Nela had figured out that the boys had no use for Luz and her long denim skirts, she had gone giddy with the flattery, laughing in the dark at even the stupidest of jokes, the boys trying hard to impress her. Even if she had met Javi then, her eyes had been on the senior boys—the boys who promised to win her stuffed animals at the ball toss, the waistbands of their boxers peeking from the top of their beige Dickies as they lifted wallets from their back pockets.

"It's okay," Javi said and then, without hesitation and much to her surprise, "you weren't my kind of girl anyway."

"You got a lot of nerve," Nela said, pushing away her food.

"It's true," he said. "What's wrong with saying the truth?"

"Why wasn't I your kind of girl?"

"Does it matter?" Javi asked. He ate, looking around vaguely, and Nela followed his eyes. He looked at none of the girls passing by, not even the junior high girls, the ones the senior boys never failed to drool over.

"You gay or something?"

"No," Javi said. "See what I mean, though? You have to find a way to put somebody down if you don't like what they say. Just like your boyfriend."

"I don't have a boyfriend."

"Lando isn't your boyfriend?"

"Lando *wasn't* my boyfriend," she corrected him, only to quickly see that she wasn't correcting him of very much.

"Call him whatever you want," Javi said, "but I think he's an asshole."

She turned to look around for Luz, to look for Alonso's slender and towering height, but it was harder now, the sun gone down to dusk and more and more people around. "I don't even know why I came."

"Hey," said Javi, "I'm sorry. I shouldn't be saying things. It's just the way you looked at me like that."

"Like what?"

"Like I wasn't good enough for you."

"You trying to be good enough for me?"

To that, Javi had no answer, but as Nela kept turning this way and that, she caught a glimpse of Lando Quintanilla. Just his shaved head turned to the side, but enough to know that it was him, enough to know that Javi was right. She wished she had been nicer to Javi then, when it sunk into her that Lando Quintanilla had brought someone with him to the carnival. Somewhere in the thickness of the crowd, he was holding someone else's hand, but there were too many people now, too many bodies, for Nela to get a good view.

"Thanks for the food," Nela said, a little sheepishly. She had been staring into the crowd too long, and when Javi didn't answer, she worried that he had spotted what had distracted her.

"The Reedley carnival has better tacos," he said, wiping his fingers. He gathered their paper plates and used napkins and rose from his seat. "You done?"

"Yeah, thanks," she said, and watched Javi as he took her trash to a nearby bin.

Lando Quintanilla surprised her, maneuvering out of the crowd and to the head of the wooden table. "Who's the fat fuck?"

Nela didn't answer him. She didn't raise her head to him either, not even to look past him, to see what girl was standing over there waiting for him.

Javi made his way back and, without saying anything to Lando Quintanilla, sat down.

"You know she has a kid, right?"

"Lando . . ." she tried.

"I'm not talking to you . . ." he said, keeping his eyes on Javi.

"Yeah, I know," said Javi. "And?"

Before Nela could say his name again, that other girl said it, an impatient plea, a hurry-up tone. She hated him for it, the way he had turned into the kind of guy whose name always had to be said out loud like that, to get him to stop, to get him to hurry up, to get him. The girl's voice called out one more time.

"This is bullshit, Nela," Lando said, but she refused to raise her head to watch him go. It took Javi speaking to know that he was long gone.

"See," said Javi. "I told you he was an asshole."

"I never said he wasn't."

"He's still looking at you."

"So why are you looking over there?" Nela asked. "I don't want any trouble with him."

"You're prettier than the girl he's with," Javi said. After a beat, he added, "She's from Reedley," and Nela stayed in that pause, a taunt to her curiosity. Her eyes took to the amber lightbulbs of the game booths, the large plush animals floating silly in the dusky sky above them. She could hear a girl shrieking in glee, the tumble of milk bottles, and she didn't have to look over to see that it was a young couple who hadn't made any of her mistakes.

"Excuse me," said Javi, but she ignored him. "Excuse me," he said again, and then again. He said it enough for Nela to realize that he wasn't even speaking to her. "Do you have a pen I can borrow?" he asked an older woman passing by, who fished in her purse and pulled one out. He grabbed a stray napkin on their table. "Give me your number," he said to Nela.

"Javi, you're sweet and everything . . ."

"Trust me on this," said Javi. "He's still looking over here."

"Why do you want trouble?"

"It's not trouble," he said, and then he started scribbling. "It's just for show anyway."

When it occurred to Nela what he was doing—what he was willing to do to give Lando Quintanilla the same gut-punch feeling she had when she had spotted that other girl—she caught a flash of Luz's beaming face breaking through the crowd, coming back with Alonso Alonso Alonso. It was time go back home.

"It's for the phone in the laundry room. We don't have one at our place."

Javi looked at her so sweetly that the embarrassment of having to admit that went away almost as it came. He noted it in a rush.

"See, I wasn't long," Luz said, her eyes on Javi as he slipped the napkin into his pocket. She let go of Alonso's arm and Alonso, staring dumbly at her, made no protest when she grabbed Nela's hand.

"You giving them a ride?" Javi asked.

"We're walking," Luz begged off, even though it was near-dark already, and she pulled Nela from the bench. For all her big talk, Nela knew that Luz feared being seen in Alonso's car, but admired the risk Luz took in briefly kissing Alonso's cheek.

"Bye, Javi," Nela said. They walked briskly home, moving through the dark but familiar streets of their neighborhood. She and Luz were doing as they pleased, but here she was, thinking of the old stories her mother told of what happened to girls in the dark. Luz shared in her hard breathing, silent. It was only when they turned the last corner and the light of the Las Palmas complex came into view that Luz spoke.

"Thanks for coming with me."

"If you wanted me to come just so you could see Alonso, you should've just said so."

"That wasn't why. You had a good time, right?"

"With Javi? Give me a break."

"He's kind of sweet, if you ask me."

As they approached Las Palmas, they could hear the soft rumble of an idling engine. They had been too far up the block to make out the parking lights. Nela knew instantly who it was.

"You should cross the street before he sees you," Nela said.

"Lando?" Luz asked. "He was there?"

It was too late to tell her about it. "I'm just going straight up the stairs and closing the door behind me," Nela told her. "So unless you want to hear him yelling, I'd just go home if I were you."

"I'll walk you to the door," Luz said.

"Go on," Nela urged and gave her a little shove to cross the road and hurry home. Almost as soon as Luz was swallowed by the dark end of the street, his voice called out, patient but demanding. "Nela . . . Nela . . ." She picked up her pace, her eyes fixed on the landing of the apartment where, to her surprise, the silhouette of her mother sat waiting.

"Nela . . ." his voice said.

Her mother rose to her feet as soon as she saw her, the bundle in her arms. She glared down at Nela as she made her way up the stairs. "He came here looking for you and what do you want me to say, huh? Huh?" Her mother spoke loudly and Nela sensed the neighbors looking out of their windows. They had been looking even before she had gotten there, drawn earlier by a man yelling, an infant crying.

"Stop moving the baby like that," she told her mother.

"Now you got two babies to take care of," her mother said. "Or maybe I got three."

"Nela . . ."

Her mother handed her the baby. "I'm not taking care of your problems for you no more. I'm just telling you." She turned to go back inside the apartment as Lando came up the stairs.

"So you just hanging out at the park now, or what?"

"Lando, go home. Like you weren't doing the same thing."

"If you let me see the baby more often . . ."

"Knock it off."

The baby started to cry.

"Who's the guy?"

"None of your business, Lando. Why do you care anyway?"

"Because it's not right."

"I don't want to argue right now. And besides, you're making the baby cry."

"Hand him over, then," Lando said. "You're the mom and you're not even holding him right. Here," he said, reaching out.

He reached out with one arm. Only one arm and that was why Nela pulled the baby closer.

"I'll show you," Lando Quintanilla said, and he took the baby from her with both hands with an ease that froze her. She was stuck in place when he calmly held the baby over the landing, its feet kicking loose over the open air.

"Nela!" She could hear Luz's voice way off in the dark.

"Ay, dios mio . . ." said someone down below.

"I swear to God, Nela, if I see you out like that with another guy, I'll hurt somebody. You hear me? You understand me?"

Her mother's door had shut against the fearful whispering down below that now grew into admonition. "¡Desgraciado!" someone finally said. Someone spoke up and Nela wished the voice had been hers. But she couldn't join them as they called out. "¡Eso no es un hombre!" When the voices yelled out for the policía, Lando Quintanilla shoved their baby back into her arms and bounded down the stairs, almost knocking over Luz at the bottom. Nela clung to the baby's fingers helplessly, her own hands useless, and tried to still its crying.

"Nela . . ." Luz said her name as if she had some explaining to do. She came up the stairs and Nela closed in on the baby, her shoulders huddled down around him. She could shield her tears from Luz, but she could not tamp down her cries, the only thing her voice could do. "Why did he do that, Nela?" Luz asked, the wrong question to the wrong person. Down below, the parking lot stayed silent, but Nela knew without looking that the neighbors were as watchful as ever, trying to figure out what had happened, why it had happened. She hated that they would see the reasons. She hated that they would talk about that girl who lived with her mother, that boy who came around to bang on their door.

From the laundry room came the ring of the telephone, endless, because no one did laundry at that hour. The phone stayed silent for a moment and then it rang again. Luz seemed not to hear it, but Nela counted each of the rings, knew the waiting behind it. Below, finally, came the shuffle of the house slippers and Doña Hortencia, rushing to the laundry room, saying "¡Córrele, córrele!" to herself. It was not the call she was expecting. It was not the right time of day. It was not the Radio Bilingüe announcer at the other end.

The phone rang once more and Nela finally raised her head, her tears dried. She saw Doña Hortencia standing in the parking lot, look-ing at the open door to the laundry room. She went in to answer the phone one more time. "¿Bueno?" Nela could hear her say. "¿Bueno?" and then her house slippers shuffled back across the concrete.

Out of the shadows, a woman came to gather her. Nela knew in-stantly that it was Doña Hortencia's mother, though she had never—not once—seen her before. The woman was old but patient. She put her arms around Doña Hortencia to lead her back home and looked up at Nela and Luz. "She confuse," the woman said, raspy and apolo-getic, but strong and loving. "She just confuse."

THE CONSEQUENCES

From the old westerns that his mother loved, Mark remembered one sound in particular: a stagecoach trundling across a landscape, the jostle of the wheels against the hard dirt road of a prairie. Those movies had always made him sleepy as a child, nestling against his mother as she watched her black-and-white television set, just the two of them in the darkened living room. The sound nearly always woke him because it meant the end of the story. Someone was leaving. Sometimes it was the villain escaping and sometimes it was a good man who had done one wrong thing. But someone was always leaving.

These days, his mother still lived in the same house, but now there was a color set and a small couch for each of them, a glass of sherry in his mother's hand. Mark had his own apartment in central Fresno and a job as a payments clerk for the water department, long lines of people waiting to argue over their bills. He was as bored with his life as his mother was lonely with hers. He would eat an evening meal with her and stay when she wanted company for the old movies. The films were always the same. Or rather, they always ended the same way, a rousing orchestra that stirred him awake from his long days.

Mark had no clue about what he really wanted and did little except wait for the weekend, when he had the energy to end the work-day at five in the afternoon on a Friday, then drive the four hours from Fresno to Los Angeles. He had lived for the neon intensity of those weekends, when the people he met exposed nothing close to unhappiness and what little money he had saved over a whole month ended up happily spilled on dance floors in the very late hours.

This was how he had met Teddy at the beginning of the year. Flushed and sweaty from dance-club drinking, he had trailed after him to an Echo Park apartment, a narrow bedroom at the end of a lonely hall. Teddy said the apartment was owned by an older man in his sixties, a man whom Mark never saw, but could hear pacing in the kitchen. The January dawn had broken through the windows, a strong light for winter, but it was the sound of Teddy gasping that had surely woken the old man. Mark had heard the pacing, had registered the old man pausing to listen to them, and had pushed into Teddy with more fervor, harder still when the quiet from the kitchen deepened. He enjoyed causing this kind of hurt, and when they released themselves into sighs and murmurs, Mark had asked Teddy to come away with him.

It was a dumb thing to ask. But he was so drunk and Teddy was so young and attractive, and so he dared himself to openly admit he wanted someone like Teddy as a boyfriend. To Mark's surprise, Teddy said yes. He had nothing keeping him in LA, Teddy said, not even the old man. What was there to leave but a string of restaurant jobs that he didn't like anyway? Mark reminded him that he lived in Fresno, that he worked as a payments clerk for the water department. Hardly a life of glamour. "You should be inviting me to live here in LA," Mark said, as if he had been waiting for just such an invitation. He had never done anything more than absently dream about leaving Fresno. He was too scared to do it.

Teddy was more drawn to the idea as they talked about it. He had come all the way from Texas and, though he had been in LA for only a few months, he was finding it expensive. Mark admired his brashness, his courage in leaving home behind. He had met plenty of people like Teddy before, but not with the same eager sweetness. "Think about it," Teddy said.

Over the next few weeks, coming and going over the Grapevine on the weekends, Mark thought about what their life together might be like. Though he couldn't imagine much more than bigger parties and newer nightclubs, he convinced himself that it was worth a shot, and by mid-February Teddy came with him back to Fresno, his belongings fitting in no more than two small suitcases.

Having Teddy around soothed some of the boredom of the Valley and they settled in with each other with not much fuss. Teddy was easy to live with, and though it took him some time to find work waiting tables in Fresno, he didn't complain about the long hours or the smaller tips. He shared what he could to help pay the rent, open with the little money that he had. He seemed, at least for a bit, relieved to be away from the noise of LA. Mark's mother sensed why he wasn't available and she eased off the drinking when Mark didn't have time to stop at the store to get her anything. He would eat dinner with her, though, at least once a week, cheerfully volunteering to stay over for a movie, but his mother would send him off with a lightness that was just as false. Teddy never even asked to meet her.

Their high times came that summer, when they stopped going to LA and drove over to San Francisco instead. It was here that Mark saw how bold Teddy was talking to strangers, introducing himself, how easily he made friends in a whole new city. Mark saw how people gravitated toward Teddy's slender beauty, the big show some of them made when they learned how far they'd driven just for a weekend. These were fast acquaintances, full of chatter and drinking and friendly gossip, but thin and brittle all the same. It was Teddy who could score them a bump of coke or Teddy who could catch

Mark's
self-deprecating

the attention of a hot stranger. As the weeks went on, Mark began to understand how people saw him—not quite the old man in LA, but ridiculous in his own way. Teddy could do much better, their glances told him. In those moments when Teddy slipped away alone in the nightclub, Mark let the worst truths wash over him. He was being used and he couldn't even fully admit it to himself.

"I don't feel like going away this weekend," he said, one Wednesday in late August. Mark expected Teddy to protest, but he was quiet about it, and when Labor Day weekend rolled around, they stayed in the Valley. Some part of him thought this would reveal Teddy's true colors, that he'd show how much he couldn't stand being in a place that reminded him of being back in Texas. "I'm waiting for you to tell me how bored to death you are," Mark said.

"But this is nice," Teddy said. "Maybe this is what I really like."

"Someone taking care of you?" Mark asked. He looked around at the small apartment, at the dusty wall heater and the windowless kitchen, and saw how little he was really offering.

Teddy looked stung. "Being together," he said. "No matter where."

"Oh, come on," Mark said. "You're too young to be saying things like that. Or maybe I'm too old."

Teddy asked him if he had ever lived with someone. "Just once," Mark said. "A girlfriend, actually. I clearly wasn't ready for anything."

"Maybe you still aren't," Teddy said. He got up and went to the bedroom, and returned with his small address book, where he kept a stash of postcards. He ignored Mark as he filled one out.

"Who you writing to?" Mark asked.

"My sister," he answered. "I'm writing her to come get me."

"Oh, really? Why don't you call her?"

"We've got our ways," Teddy answered and then his face crumpled. "I can count on her," he said, beginning to cry, and then told Mark about being ill, that he'd been ill for a while, and that it was time to start thinking about who he could really trust.

This was the moment, Mark knew, when maybe Teddy expected him to say that he was the one to trust, but it wasn't true. Men like Teddy were all over the newspapers and a small but terrible part of Mark wondered if Teddy was lying about it. Mark reached over for the address book and Teddy kept his attention on his postcard. He saw the names of Lucho and Fabiana Contreras and an address in Texas, carefully printed in Teddy's neat handwriting. It was the small town that Teddy swore he'd never see again, an address he surely knew by heart, but it made Mark realize that Teddy had written it down for others to find it if they ever needed it.

A week passed. The postcard had gone out, but Mark had not made it his business to know if it was an explanation or an apology, a plea or a confession. The sister didn't come, but Mark wasn't surprised. From another room, Mark could hear Teddy going through the trouble of spinning out a long-distance number on the rotary phone, but never heard a conversation. The blaze of their San Francisco summer weekends was hardly even a memory. He couldn't tell if Teddy was planning to leave or only making a show of it. Furtively, Mark visited a clinic to get himself tested, and in the impatient days that he waited for the result, Mark was more angry than afraid of the possibility. He was ready to blame Teddy for everything. But when the test came back negative, his relief gave way to even more suspicion. He wanted his old life back, as boring as it was, and Teddy could sort out his problems on his own.

"You need to start thinking about going home," Mark said. "If you're really sick," he added.

"Why would anybody lie about something like that?" Teddy asked. He reddened with anger, with deep hurt, but he didn't lash out, which made Mark understand how wounding his words were. He really was ill.

distrustful

A few days later, they ended their short time together at the bus station in downtown Fresno. Teddy allowed Mark to drive him over and wait for the bus departure. He watched Teddy count out the bills at the ticket booth, how long it must have taken to save up the money to get back to Texas. He hadn't offered to help and Teddy hadn't asked. The bus station was sparse, only single men from Mexico loitering about with no family waiting for them. Even at midafternoon, when the bus was ready to board, Teddy was the only passenger. "I'm really sorry," he told Teddy as he hugged him good-bye, but Teddy only closed his eyes and shrugged. He got on the bus and, as he turned into the aisle to take his seat, his slender frame was lost instantly behind the dark windows. They hadn't known each other long enough to learn how they might have been in better times or with more trivial problems, but something kept Mark standing there as the bus pulled out. Something moved him to wave at the dark windows without knowing for sure if Teddy was looking back out at him.

That should have been the end of it, Teddy on his way back to Texas. For almost an hour after the bus left, Mark stayed at the bus station, as aimless as the men milling about. He took his inability to move for sadness but when he closed his eyes, he could hardly picture the details of Teddy's face. At most, he thought, this feeling would last another few days until Teddy got back to Texas. He could try out another apology for the phone call he expected when Teddy finally arrived. He would be sincere and honest then.

But the phone call didn't come. The words that Mark rehearsed grew distant and vague and he found himself waiting for the mail, certain that a postcard with a message from Teddy would show up, but nothing. The weeks went on. As autumn shortened the days, Mark understood he would never hear from Teddy again.

Thanksgiving neared. "You seem more tired than usual," his mother said. "Should we cook a turkey dinner?" she asked, but he didn't answer her. On the day itself, he drove over in apologetic silence and the two of them had a joyless early meal at a chain restaurant on Belmont Avenue, the tables taken up by elderly couples. At one table, a lone customer reminded Mark of the old man in Los Angeles, though he'd never seen him, and he struggled to remember if Teddy had even said goodbye to him when he left the Echo Park apartment.

Afterward, they stopped at a Longs drugstore just before it closed for his mother to buy a bottle of cream sherry. They lounged in front of her television set until *The Wizard of Oz* came on. The sepia tones of the opening put him in mind of Teddy traveling some great, uncrossable distance and when his mother nodded off, Mark quietly rose to the rotary phone. He whispered the names of Lucho and Fabiana Contreras to the operator, who grew impatient with him. "Could you speak up, sir?" she asked. "What is the name of the town again, sir?" she said, forceful enough that Mark feared his mother would wake and he set the receiver back in the cradle.

His mother took to inviting him over for dinner more frequently or asking for an errand to be run. She tried this on a Saturday but Mark let the phone ring and ring. It went silent, but five minutes later, it rang one more time, as if to make sure.

And so it was that Mark, boxed in by the lack of news from Texas, found himself doing exactly what he had seen Teddy do in the weeks before he left: he sat on the edge of his bed and called a number in Texas, the line buzzing without end. As Teddy had done, he counted to twenty through the endless ringing. One, one thousand, two. All the way to the sad pause before trying again.

"There's no way I can tell you that, sir," another operator explained to him, when Mark asked to confirm if the number he had taken from his long-distance bill was indeed listed to Lucho and Fabiana Contreras. The operator told him so in a much kinder voice—it was getting closer to Christmas and maybe she understood that there were many people asking for reassurance in the guise of information. "Would you like to try again?"

When the new year came, Mark decided to let the matter go, a resolution of sorts. The January fog made it hard to drive out of the Valley for a weekend and the one time Mark did, the clubs in San Francisco were empty and lackluster. None of the names that Mark had collected on matchbooks and deli napkins seemed to ring true of anyone he had actually known. He cut his visit short. He drove back to the Valley with some edge of dread about old habits and when the road from the coastal foothills slowly enveloped him back into the dreariness of the winter fog, Mark knew he was in for it.

He called, then again another day, waited some, then tried once more. Every time, the phone buzzed without ending and every time he got closer to counting twenty, he felt himself sink. And then, on the last day of January, just as he was thinking of how the new month might shake him out of this dullness, the line broke through to a crackle. On the other end, he could hear someone fumble with the receiver.

"¿Bueno?" asked a woman, low and tired and raspy.

Mark was so surprised that his throat caught and before he could say anything, the woman hung up. He tried again, but no one answered.

He sat on the bed, looking at the phone and wondering if he had spoken to Fabiana Contreras and before he could let go of the moment as merely a crossed connection, he tried once more.

This time, on the first ring, the call was answered. A younger woman this time, her voice forceful and demanding. "Hello?"

"Hello," Mark answered.

"Is this who I think it is?" she asked.

All he remembered of Teddy's talk of Texas was nothing. "Nothing's there," Teddy had said, then told him about sugar beets and dust. Fieldwork and food stamps. The one high school and no place to hide. The Gulf Coast in one direction, the plains in the other. Salt in the air one day, manure the next. Skinny streets and too many churches. The single gas station and the hospital thirty miles away. The bingo hall and a lot of American flags. A town full of nothing and somehow devoid of family.

"Who is this?" the young woman asked again.

"It's me," Mark said, though he did not know what he was admitting to.

There was a long pause on the other end of the line. He knew what the silence meant but, mercifully, it did not darken out to the hiss of a dropped call. He heard the young woman swallow hard.

"He's gone," she said. "He left us yesterday morning."

His fiance Teddy died

"I'm so sorry," Mark stammered. He had overheard his mother say those words on the telephone to her newly widowed friends and he had thought, at the time, that the words were a relief to her. She had been alone for so long and the words echoed in her kitchen walls as a reciprocal comfort, as something she had been waiting a long time to say.

The young woman didn't respond. "When is the funeral?" Mark asked.

"It's for family only," she said, and he knew then that she was Teddy's sister. An older sister, because he couldn't picture Teddy being anyone but the youngest in a family. "Goodbye," she said and the familiar buzz that had haunted him all winter came again.

The next day was Sunday. Mark drove over to his mother's early in the morning to take her to church. He dropped her off and then waited at a coffee shop on Shaw Avenue, absently flipping the newspapers past stories of workers striking in Poland, the closing of a Renault factory in France. The reality of their distances became clear to him, the world so far away from the fogged-out streets of Fresno. The chill stayed in the air all morning and he knew the weather would keep some of the churchgoers away. He would have to be prompt in picking up his mother after. No one would be there to keep her company, to talk to her about the news of the day, though he was certain none of those people cared much about Poland or France.

His mother stood alone on the empty front steps of the church and began moving toward the car almost as soon as she saw it. She was eager to talk, but saw that Mark was not in the mood for conversation. She picked up the newspaper and scanned the pages even more quickly than he had. "They're Catholics over in Poland, aren't they?" she asked, but didn't wait for an answer. "It's so dreary today," she said, looking at the weather report. "All week it's going to be like this, but it'll change. You'll see," she said, putting her gloved hand on his and leaving it there.

The fog made the car ride even quieter and when they turned on to her street, she invited him to dinner. "I'll make a soup, something to warm your blood."

Mark said neither yes nor no, but when his mother got out of the car, she said, "See you around seven," before closing the door. He watched her huddle to the front of her house, preoccupied with her keys, and knew this was the most he could reasonably demand of her.

He napped for the rest of the afternoon, his apartment gone dark by the time he opened his eyes again, and when he turned on the light, his room felt meager and bare, the day wasted in sleep. Tomorrow would be Monday and the workweek would begin, dreary weather or not. Things would continue, whether he was ready for them or not.

This was why putting on his shoes to go to his mother's felt aimless but inevitable at the same time, why the drizzle in the air emerging from the fog chilled him even deeper. Mark drove to his mother's house and it was impossible to warm up when he arrived. She noticed his hunched posture and promptly ladled out a bowl of sausage and greens. Their dinner was quiet and she didn't pry.

To cheer herself, she turned to the Sunday comedies. When Mark made motions to depart, she convinced him to stay when the hand-claps to *The Jeffersons* came on. His mother liked the sassy maid and she poured herself a glass of sherry, prepared to lose herself in the lull of light jokes. To their surprise, it was a more somber episode in which Louise Jefferson, finding out that the drab building she grew up in had been slated for demolition, pays it one last visit. It was an episode of reminiscence and Mark's mother hardly laughed. Their shared quiet made the disappointment larger still. Mark thought about why television shows did this now and again, the comedies shading deep and sometimes sinister. Everyone had a past, he supposed. Everyone had to be granted the dignity of a past. Louise Jefferson had a sister, he learned, someone named Maxine, who had long ago run off. Louise Jefferson had a mother, testy and rushing offstage to grab a belt for punishment. The adult Louise, thinking about the consequences, seemed none the worse for remembering. She was reminding herself that she had been a good daughter, that her mother had told her so on her wedding day. She had a goodness in her, her mother told her, and she might one day understand that when she had children, how you don't love them all the same.

The studio audience hushed in acknowledgment when Louise glimpsed the glass doorknobs of her childhood bedroom. She had dreamed of them as diamonds once but now she had risen above and so she unscrewed them, slipping them into her coat, the audience murmuring their approval. The past didn't work that way, Mark thought. It was sentimental and cheap to think you could tuck anything away like a jewel for safekeeping, something to pull out and admire.

When Mark began to wonder if his mother had fallen asleep, she rose from the couch to pour herself another glass of sherry. "She'll be all better next week," his mother said, and when she sat down again, Mark took his leave.

His mother was correct. Next week, they would watch a fresh

misunderstanding, the maid ready with her stinging quips. Most people would forget about the sister Maxine, would forget that she had ever been mentioned, why she had run away, and where she had gone to. He mulled over this on his way home, the ease by which such seriousness could be erased. But the pattern of his daily life had not erased Teddy. He took the same streets home, but when he got to Clovis Avenue, he turned right, heading toward the 99 South. Los Angeles lay just four hours away, maybe even closer because it was a Sunday night and the drizzle kept the traffic even thinner. Nothing impeded him. He moved along the highway on impulse and it was only in Bakersfield that he stopped to buy a road map at a gas station. He studied the single line of his destination, the road he knew into the heart of Los Angeles, and then all the ones out of it, to places he did not know. He picked the one moving all the way east and drove on.

The interstate took him to the endless edge of Los Angeles, its suburbs blurring along hour after hour. Near dawn, the density of the buildings broke away and the road cut through rough stretches of desert, the lamplights gone and the cars fewer. The road grew lonelier and Mark found himself anxious for the sun to rise, afraid of what he was doing and the mindless way he had gone about it.

But when the sun did rise, the severity of the landscape astonished him, the black rock and the cacti, the bare and scraggly trees, the way he could see the wind carry itself along the sand. In his imagination, all of Arizona and New Mexico would be like this and Texas not much better. Mark felt all the worse for sending anyone on such a long road alone, worse still when he thought of the escape Teddy had made once before, from the other direction.

At a busy truck stop, he ate a heavy plate of eggs and bacon, his waitress sensing that he was rushed but exhausted. "I don't think you've got much driving left in you," she said to him and, in the parking lot, Mark closed his eyes for a moment. The drone of the trucks and the hiss of their brakes steadied to a lull. When he woke, it was afternoon and the light was sharp but gentle, the built-up heat in the car good for the chill that had crept into his bones in Fresno.

He drove on and the cities drew greater spaces between them. The farther he went, the more quickly he wanted to arrive, and he made his stops as short as possible. Late into evening, he crossed the Texas border at a little town called Van Horn and signs all along the interstate warned him about the last great distance before the next town. "Nighttime isn't a good time to take that road," the gas station manager told him. "You break down, there's nothing out there. Nothing, nothing, nothing."

Mark kept looking out at the black nothing that lay just beyond the gas station, the black nothing that Teddy had come from, and the black nothing into which he had returned.

depressing [handwritten margin note]

He must have looked too long into it because the gas station manager spoke with new urgency. "Just get a bite to eat and rest up for the morning," he said, "before it gets too late." He directed Mark to the one diner in town that was still open and the waitress took an interest in him. It was late and most of the truck drivers had taken their meals and gone to rest for the night. Janelle wanted to know where he was going and who he was going to see and where he came from. Mark found himself lying. Corpus Christi, he said, from Albuquerque, to see his girlfriend, and this kept Janelle's questions short and defeated. She went back to wiping the tables, from one end of the diner to the other, and when she was done, he thought she would come back to make more small talk. But she only stood at the register, looking past the dark windows as if she could see something others never could.

He had planned to sleep in the car, but the enormity of the dark sky and its impenetrable quiet frightened him. The nothingness prompted him to count his money and rent a room at a dingy motel. Mark rested on the rough bedspread, not even taking off his shoes, and was alarmed at the swiftness with which sleep threatened to overtake him. He resisted it straight into dream and he could see himself from above the bed, open and surrendered to the world. He could see the thin door to the motel and a light grew under it before it opened. A dark silhouette stood there against the light for a long time before he realized he could command it. "Teddy," he whispered. "Teddy, come to me," because he half-hoped that by saying his name, a needed comfort would come.

The silhouette moved toward him, but the face remained in shadow. When it refused to reveal itself, a great sadness overtook Mark and he woke, startled and tearful, to the thin motel-room door still closed, the bare lamplight, and his shoes still on.

When Mark woke again, it was well past noon. In the haze of his exhaustion, he wondered if he should call his mother. She wouldn't expect him until the weekend. He wondered about his boss, incessantly calling from the water department because it was Monday. Had it been Monday? He had lost track of the days. His stomach soured at coffee and he got back on the road without anything to eat. Slowly, the towns came quicker. The land softened, running in green streaks off the thinnest of streams. The single-pump gas stations, the brick-front pharmacies, the water towers with their bold declarations of place. SEGOVIA, read one. JUNCTION, read another.

Teddy's hometown would look exactly like these, Mark knew, as it got closer to dusk. In the distance, the glow of San Antonio shimmered in a way he had not seen light do for many miles. A beacon, but not one bright enough for all that Teddy had wanted to flee. The city disappeared from the interstate almost as rapidly as it had flickered into view and Mark continued on into darkness. When night came full on, he finally saw the name of the town—MATHIS, stark and singular on a green sign—and counted the last long miles before pulling over to a gas station.

A young woman sat behind the till, her hands in the pockets of her sweatshirt to keep warm, her booth protected by a scratched partition. She took his money for the gas and stared back at him with suspicion while he stood flipping through a copy of the local paper. He didn't know what he was looking for, really, once he failed to find an obituary of any kind. So he knocked on her partition and held up the paper.

"A friend of mine . . ." Mark started to tell her, but her face remained so impassive, so impatient for him to move on and leave her back in the lonely fluorescence of the booth that he couldn't finish. She couldn't be bothered to care about Teddy, about someone who had dared to escape, only to be drawn irrevocably back home, back to the blanched-out pavement of his little town.

"Hey," he said, "what's your name?" he asked, thinking it was better to start again, better to start with a name at least, the better to know any person.

"You need me to call the cops?" the young woman said. She said it with no real fear in her voice, with a belief that terrible things never happened in small towns.

"Do you know the Contreras family?" he blurted out.

A look of understanding swept her face, but only for a moment. "Their son died," she said, matter-of-factly, and pressed no further, as if she refused to make anything of Mark's bleary eyes, his sour clothing.

"I know," he said. "I drove here for his funeral. From California."

The young woman looked over at his car, her hands back in her pockets, glancing at his license plate. When she looked back at him, he saw something for the first time in a stranger's face, that he was someone who might have mattered to someone else, even in a small way. "The funeral is tomorrow morning," she said. "Their church is over on Nueces Street," she told him, and gave him the simple directions.

Mark waved his hand in feeble thanks. He pulled out of the gas

— that's sweet

station and left its dull light behind. The street thinned out to gravel, his headlights sweeping over the fallen chain-link fences and the overgrown grass that made up the neighborhood yards. He could not see the houses, only their dark shapes, the people quiet within them, not even the porch lights on. The sound of his car brought the drawing of a curtain every now and again, a silhouette looking out at him. The quiet surrounded him. He rumbled across a set of train tracks and wondered if trains ever passed through, since there was nothing to take and nothing, it seemed, had ever been delivered.

When he found the church, he pulled to the back of its parking lot and quickly shut off the engine. The white walls of the tiny building gleamed even in the dark. The shape of its cross over the threshold stood out in relief against the sky. Mark pushed the seat back and closed his eyes but the mesquite trees gave him no rest. The branches clacked against each other in the wind, empty, and if he had grown up here, if he had known the sound deep into his bones, it might have lulled him to sleep.

All night he listened to the gaunt branches. He stared at the stars and watched them give out meekly to dawn. As the sun rose, he could see that the church needed a new paint job, that its foundation sank low, that its lone swamp cooler was enough for only a few pews. The sunlight grew and the birds chirped alive, a few work trucks chugging along the streets just as they did back in Fresno. Then the morning grew quiet again, as if this was all the activity that the town could muster.

And then a black car arrived, then another, then one that had the name of a funeral home painted modestly on the door. Mark watched people get out of the cars, a tall white man getting out of a rusty Toyota and slipping past all of them to a side entry into the church. Mark spotted an older woman walking slowly and with her head down and a man who seemed shrunken by her grief holding her firmly by the arm. Their feet shuffled against the gravel. From far away, the man looked like Teddy, older and bowed.

They wore black, most of them, the thirteen people that Mark could count. Two younger teenagers wore sneakers, their feet growing too quickly for expensive dress shoes. A thinly angelic woman, her dark hair in a tight bun, motioned people along in the habit of an older sister, and soon the men and the two teenagers gathered at the vehicle from the funeral home. They lifted the casket and pulled the weight into the church.

When the parking lot cleared, Mark got out of his car. He walked to the door of the church, certain that he would go inside, but he remained on the low steps. The little sign in front of the church crowded its verse in plastic letters: He Will Cover You with His Feathers, and Under His Wings You Will Find Refuge. Up close, Mark could see that the white paint had chipped terribly. The houses of the neighborhood all shared the same, sun-blasted fate, the trees too low for shade. There was no refuge here, nowhere that Teddy could have possibly turned.

The church seemed sealed shut, but Mark took the round doorknob in his hand and opened as gently as he could. The hinges creaked but none of the thirteen heads turned around, not even the teenagers. The tall white man was at the head of the pews and he spoke in a slow English, as if he knew some people could not understand him. The black-haired heads all bowed to listen. Mark kept the door open just a bit, just enough for the tall white man to see him, just enough for the older sister to notice that the tall white man was looking at him, just enough for her to get up and order him to go away. But none of them moved and the tall white man kept talking.

He was telling them the story of Lazarus. The head of the woman who was Teddy's mother and the head of the man who was Teddy's father stayed rigid and unmoved. "Jesus called his name three times," the tall white man said, but Mark turned away from the

door. He looked out at the dilapidated houses, out to the flat and un-
promising horizons, and knew that Teddy had hated the cruelty of
these stories, too.

"Nothing is promised," said the tall white man. Mark could
hear him through the slender crevice of the door opening. "Not
tomorrow or even the next hour, and we thank you, Lord, for your
reminder to live as best we can, wrapped in your embrace, no matter the trouble." Mark could feel the heat of the tiny room seeping through the crack of the open door and he turned to face it
again. The casket stood to the right, a simple vase of white carnations on top of it.

"It may be hard to lift your head and lift your hands in thanks
today, but that's what the Lord asks you to do," the man said. He
raised his arms in praise and closed his eyes. "I want you to lift your
hands for Teodoro Contreras. Lift your hands in thanks. For the
days he gave you. For the smiles he gave you. For the way he said
good morning. For the way he said goodnight. For being a good son
to you. For being a good brother."

The tall white man stood with his arms raised and his eyes closed
but the thirteen heads stayed bowed. He spoke in slower English but
still no one moved in understanding. His eyes stayed shut to their
stillness and he beseeched them. "Lift your hearts," he said. "Even if
he failed you, his flesh and blood failed you, as we are all bound to
fail. But with the power of the blood of the Lord Jesus Christ . . ."

One of the teenagers put his hands up and the tall white man
thanked him. "Thank you," he repeated, when the other teenager
raised his arms, too, and he let the tiny room go quiet, all the heads
bowed.

Mark turned away from them, from the quiet, from the pleading. He left the door open to continue listening and sank to the low
steps when the silence only grew. He began to weep. He hadn't loved
Teddy and yet now he did. He deserved this feeling.

The tiny room stayed silent and he could not hear how the tall white man was ministering his final comfort. No sound came through and he pictured all the bowed heads waiting to be released with a last word. Mark bowed his head when he heard the shuffle of the people inside, the pews creaking from the release of their weight. His tears dropped down to the splintered wood of the low steps. In the old movies, when someone galloped into the wide distance of their redemptions, someone always tried to follow after. Someone always tried to stop them with a name shouted into echo. Someone always tried to urge them not to go with a hand up to the sky. His shoulders ached from the drive, but Mark raised his arms. He could hear the people coming outside and they would see him waiting on the low steps of a sad little church in Mathis, Texas. They got closer to the door and he stiffened his arms and held them even higher, his head bowed and his eyes closed. He could sense them begin to pass, their best shoes against the low wood, but no one said a word to him. He knew that no one would. Mark opened his hands. Then he opened them wider.

COMPROMISOS

Mauricio would stop and buy the oranges on his way back into town. He would need them as a treat for his young daughter, Rocío. She had the unfortunate gift of sensing unease in a silent room and he had to appease her. Last August, right at the start of third grade, he was sent to pick her up from school and Rocío noticed the stricken look on his face as he drove. She had seen it, but not understood it. At home, his daughter could hear how angry and hurt her mother was, but she understood only that it meant Mauricio would not stay at the house any longer, that her father would come only every few days. Even now, deep into January, Mauricio didn't know exactly what Alba had told the kids. Their older son, Alonso, was in high school with his own troubles, and if he missed having Mauricio around, he never let on. Rocío was different. Since December, Mauricio had had restless nights, sitting up in the thin bed of the one-room he was renting in Kingsburg, one town over. The hours got later and later, closer and closer to dawn, and he couldn't shake the sense that he had made a terrible mistake. The restlessness had decided for him. He would have to come back. He would have to ask forgiveness.

On the morning he decided to ask Alba to let him back, the January fog had not lifted, and he had to wait, along with everyone, for the density to break. The Saturday traffic was slow and heavy and impatient, people late for their second-job shifts, their errands. On days like this, he knew, no one would have time to stop for the old Mexican woman who sold the smallest of the winter oranges from under a white tent at one of the rural intersections outside of town. She would stand near the edge of the road sometimes, waving for customers to come, which they did out of pity or loyalty. "Mírala," Alba used to say, before they had kids, on their way to spend the day walking the Fulton Mall in Fresno. "That's going to be me one day," she said, "when it's all over."

"She's somebody's mother," Mauricio would say, which was the kind of thing they said to each other as a private reminder to be kind to those around them. This is why Alba had married him, he knew, why they had started dating in the first place. Alba had sensed in him that same dutiful nature that made her the responsible one of three girls in her family, just as pretty as her chola sisters, who lived for cruising Mooney Boulevard in Visalia, their mother always yelling at them. He knew what it meant, even way back then when they were in high school and had only coins in their pockets, to pull over at the white tent and buy the old woman's last bag of summer fruit.

This morning, though, the old woman wasn't there. When Mauricio pulled to the side of the road, the figure rising from behind the stand was a young man in a black jacket, reaching for a paper bag in anticipation. "¿Cuántas?" the young man asked, even before Mauricio reached the stand—not unkindly, but it was clear he already wanted to be done with the slow morning. The oranges were small and hail-scarred and the two crates were near full. "Media docena," Mauricio answered and he watched the young man count out six oranges for him, pushing past the ones that didn't look bright or plump enough. He saw, at the foot of the young man's chair, a plastic bucket with pink carnations.

"¿Se venden?" he asked, pointing at the flowers. It was too early in the year for flowers, but the nurseries must have started sending them out for the high school fundraisers. He could picture the cheerleaders at the basketball games with handfuls of them, the boys saving their money because this was how to show love. The more you gave, the more it mattered.

The young man raised the bucket to the table and shuffled the stems, the pink carnations already a little limp. "¿Para su señora?" he asked. He had a handsome face, now that Mauricio could study it closely, distracted as the young man was in handling the flowers, clean-shaven, his cheeks a little rough and ashy from the chill of being outside. He counted a half dozen as if he had already decided for Mauricio, his hand on another stem, hopeful.

"Sí," Mauricio said, but he was responding to the young man's face, the young man's insistence, a decision made for him without him even agreeing, as decisions had always been. Hadn't it been that way in dating Alba in high school, a pairing that sometimes felt like it had been willed by everyone else around them? Hadn't it been that way with Pico, the man from the beginning of summer, who did nothing but ask Mauricio questions undercut with gentle urging. "¿Un trago?" Pico had asked him. "Anda . . . un trago," he decided for him, just one drink, from behind the counter at the Woolworth's on Fulton Mall, handing Mauricio his purchase without ever having asked, like this young man had, if it was for his señora. Pico hadn't cared. Pico had probably seen his wedding band, but hadn't bothered to look at it again, his eyes locked on Mauricio the moment he had entered the store.

"¿Algo más?" The young man slid the bag of oranges across the table, along with the flowers, and this time he did sound unkind, aware of how Mauricio had been studying him and how much he didn't appreciate it. Mauricio shook his head and the young man quoted him the price—Mauricio knew it was too much, but he couldn't refuse now, not with the way the young man stared at him. He fumbled the money across the table, realizing only when he started toward the car that he had forgotten his change. He felt himself rush to the car, turning hurriedly toward town but seeing the young man out of the corner of his eye, one last time, hands back in his pockets.

"¿Algo más?" Pico had asked the same thing at the Woolworth's, but Mauricio had heard it differently then. It wasn't meant to rush him along, but to draw him forward. Maybe this lotion, Pico suggested, never once saying it was for any señora. The Woolworth's cosmetics counter was hardly more than a single case with nothing expensive in it, but Pico had come from behind it just the same to show some things to the man who had wandered in from the open walkways of the Fulton Mall. Men walked past the windows all day and Pico must have known how to spot the ones like Mauricio, and he knew how to speak to them in Spanish, the better to suggest something that was already understood. "Anda," Pico had urged, and Mauricio only resisted the invitation by staying in front of the counter, a dumb smile on his face. He had waited for Pico to clock out at five and they walked on the shaded side of the Fulton Mall. Even for late May, it was already scorching. People lingered on the benches and the edges of the central fountain, cooling off. Their eyes followed Pico. Out in the sunlight, Mauricio could see that Pico's hair was brassy from a dye job. He could complete the picture that the eyes all around them were forming—one boyfriend picking up the other after work, Woolworth's badge dangling from the fingers of the younger one, a small gift tucked under the arm of the other. A drink didn't seem right anymore.

"Come," Mauricio ordered, turning west when they hit the edge of the mall and they walked by the Canada shoe store and the Mexican record shop to the Crest cinema on the corner. "The movie's already started," the young woman in the booth said, looking at both of them for a moment before sliding the tickets through the mousehole. The lobby was empty by then, the carpet muffling everything except the bubbling juice fountain and the hum of the air-conditioning. Mauricio felt more at ease and they made their way past the closed double doors into the theater, where, eyes adjusting to the sudden darkness, he felt Pico's small hand reach out for his in the dark as they sought out seats in the back. He couldn't tell how many people were in the theater—not many though, and so he let Pico's hand remain in his, too soft to the touch and damp from the walk outside. It was a loud comedy, a Mexican pratfaller whose name he couldn't remember, and in the clatter of overturned restaurant tables and policemen slipping into muddy street puddles and a loudmouth kid who made the dark theater choke with laughter, Mauricio felt Pico's hand reach over to his belt buckle, his fingers unzipping his pants and slipping inside. Did it matter if the dark theater could hear the squeak of the vinyl seats, the Woolworth's bag crinkling? At first, Mauricio thought it did—it did matter—two men who walked into a theater in the middle of the day, one of them with brassy, dyed hair, the other one older and who should know better. But then it didn't matter, and the hinges of his chair creaked as he spread his legs and let Pico do what he wanted. When Pico felt him start to come, he gripped Mauricio harder and let out a little laugh of triumph, a giggle almost. Mauricio moved to get Pico's hand out of his pants, afraid someone would finally turn around to see them, but Pico held firm, drawing his fingers around the stickiness and grinning at him. Nothing was funny on the screen, but it didn't matter. That's how life was, Mauricio thought, the things that brought some people to laughter.

Pico sent him home after that, a mess in his pants even after he went into the theater bathroom and wiped himself clean. He knew he'd see Pico again. Or try to. The summer went on like that, the drives to Fresno longer and longer, and Alba, he knew, reluctant to ask him questions, her back turned to him at night with a deep sigh. What did it matter? he kept asking himself. He had one answer in his children. "I'm somebody's father," he said aloud to himself, in the darkness of his one-room in Kingsburg, trying to remind himself of parental pride, the joy in children that everyone claimed, but he couldn't feel it deep down. He would never say so. Some things shouldn't be asked. He could sense a better question in Pico, a truer answer at a back table at La Fiesta, where the bartender warmly poured them drinks and left them alone in the dark shadow of the nearly empty bar. "No, no, no," Pico had said, when Mauricio dared to let slip what he had been thinking about. Mauricio had it all wrong. "You already made your bed," Pico told him. "I'm not asking you to leave anybody."

Pico didn't mention it again, but he had been firm enough, and it reminded Mauricio that he had, in fact, made a decision a long time ago. It had been a bad one, he knew now. To think that marriage could settle him into the calm he knew he needed, that it would help him rise over his own dishonesty. He didn't have the courage to ask Pico if it was his marriage or the children that he saw as an uncrossable line. He knew Pico would never offer more than drinks at a back table at La Fiesta. He could listen to Pico talk about the night classes he was scheduled to take at the community college during the summer session or the trip that he was saving for to visit his mother in Los Mochis, right on the coast in Sinaloa. But they were Pico's plans, only his. He didn't talk about them in a way that invited Mauricio to even imagine about sharing in them.

So he knew, then, that he didn't have anywhere else to go. As he approached the house, he saw Alba spot the car from the living room window, perplexed to see him driving up on a Saturday morning. He watched her silhouette move into the kitchen to greet him from the side door of the house—she didn't like him using the front door anymore, where the kids would know immediately that he had arrived. At the side door, she could speak low to him if things turned harsh, or block him out entirely if an argument threatened to erupt. She could study his manner, the look on his face, and figure out if she was up for anything that took too much effort. She'd grown wary now, when, back in high school, she had been the timid one, clerking at the furniture store on Tulare Street. Mauricio had gotten to know her after he'd been hired part time for deliveries, going up to the front counter with signed charge slips that she needed to stamp and file away. In those brief encounters, Alba would smile timidly at him, and it was something that he knew what to do with—an interest that he wouldn't have to act on. She was years from knowing the truth about him, years from being able to see through him.

So when he parked the car and saw Alba already standing at the threshold of the side door to the house, he didn't reach for the carnations. He left them sitting on the passenger seat. He took only the bag of oranges, tucking them under his arm as if they were just a newspaper, but he could see Alba's eyes trained on it, judging whether or not he could come into the house. The closer he got, the sharper her look became, her eyes so trained on the bag that he sensed that it was his heart in judgment. She was in no mood to make any guesses, he could tell, so he held the bag out to her, his arms outstretched.

"What's this?" Alba asked, not moving from the threshold, the door behind her as if he were a vacuum salesman.

To answer her simply, with just the one word—Mauricio knew what it sounded like, the thinness of his intentions. So he stood like that, reaching out for the long moment it took Alba to accept the bag, open it, and look inside. She was judging him and maybe she had the right to do so, but as she peered into the bag, he couldn't help but notice that the resentment on her face had no trace of the fact that she, too, had once left the marriage for a small stretch. It had been a surprise, very early on, before the kids. She had taken up with Nepo, who worked for city garbage collection. Nepo had been several years ahead of them in high school, but Mauricio hardly remembered him. That was how big the town was—people measured themselves by the years they did or didn't go to high school and the circles they ran in. Only Nepo's name was memorable to him. Not what Nepo looked like or if he was in a marriage or if he had kids or why Alba had gotten together with him at all. She was gone only two months and she quit Nepo before she could fall in too deep. "Out of respect," Alba had said, "for my vows." She had humbled herself in apology when she said that, hands crossed at the kitchen table, head bowed. And maybe this was why she scowled at Mauricio now for returning on a Saturday morning, blocking the door and his view into the house in case their daughter wandered into the kitchen. Maybe this was why she saw the oranges and knew what he was trying to do.

"Lookit . . ." she said, sounding just like her chola sisters, the ones who had told her from the beginning that he wasn't the man she thought he was. Giggles, one of them went by, and La Troubles, the one who could do nothing but complain. "Lookit," Alba said, "I mean it when I say I just want you to be happy."

She didn't even give him a chance to speak. Maybe it was better that he didn't say aloud what he felt he should say, but knew wasn't true. *If you want me to come back*, he had decided to say, sitting on the edge of his bed at dawn. *For the kids.* Self-sacrifice was deeper than love, he had thought, and maybe Alba would recognize that. Mauricio had felt so sure, but facing Alba now, the door still half-closed behind her, he couldn't explain himself anymore and didn't know what to do.

"You don't need to ruin your life," Pico had told him. "You just need to live it."

From the kitchen, he could hear the footsteps of their young daughter coming into the kitchen, stopping to contemplate who was at the door. Alba closed the door a little tighter behind her.

"Listen," she said, lowering her voice. "Why don't you go pick up Alonso for me? He's rehearsing for a quinceañera right now at the Veterans' Hall."

He nodded at her, knowing not to say anything to alert their daughter to the sound of his voice. Alba slipped behind the door and shut it quickly behind her. He didn't know if she wanted him to simply drop Alonso off, if she wanted to talk things over or not. Maybe it wasn't something to settle in one conversation. The gesture was everything, he decided, a first step at least. He drove over to the Veterans' Hall, where, noticing that no other parents were waiting in their cars, he guessed he had arrived too early. He made his way to the long lobby entrance, where a woman holding a bucket and a damp rag pointed at one of the benches. "It's dry," she said. "It's clean," she said, "if you want to sit down." Mauricio nodded at her and sat down to wait. He could hear the faint footsteps of a group practicing their dance steps in the main room, and the woman continued her patient work of wiping down the scratched, lacquered wood of the benches, of the display cases with medals and American flags. She moved slowly through the length of the long lobby, the brick walls faded and chipped, her hand moving the damp rag in a reverent circle over the bronze plaques and the framed pictures of all the hometown boys who had come and gone. She was a widow— she had to be, Mauricio decided, of someone in one of the black-and-white pictures on the wall—for her to dutifully clean what no one ever really noticed. A trace of Pine-Sol lingered in the air and it reminded him of the faint smell of the back of La Fiesta, the bar dark and secret, but here the lobby was filled with winter light. Something was amiss, Mauricio thought, and it took a moment for him to realize it was the sound of the dance steps, the faint offbeat of someone out of sync.

He rose from the bench and peered through the skinny window in the door leading to the main room. There was Alonso, in a pink vest and bow tie, the girls in wide, full ball gowns. Like the rest of the boys, he was having trouble maneuvering the dance steps with all of that fabric.

"The main girl's not even there." The cleaning woman had joined him at the door, peering through the glass. "Which one is yours?"

"The tall skinny boy," he said. He could see what girls liked about Alonso, his height wobbling him, his head a little too big and his shoulders too narrow, but steady somehow, sure of himself.

"Ah," said the cleaning woman. "He looks like you." They watched the group move through the routine, Alonso the only boy to get the dance steps correct that time. "He's good," she said. "He's got a right and left."

"You know what time their rehearsal is over?"

"Soon," she said. "They've been at it for a while. And you know teenagers can't do anything for very long if they get bored." She turned back to her cleaning and, not long after, disappeared from the lobby altogether. Mauricio watched the group rehearse, Alonso focused enough to not notice that he was being watched by his father. Mauricio returned to the bench to wait. He could hear the footsteps echo in the lobby, now that he had nothing else to focus on, and he could hear the lack of unison. He thought he could almost hear the sighs of frustration as they had to work through it one more time.

At the entrance, two girls walked into the lobby. One girl wore a long denim skirt—a church girl—and she held open the door long enough for her friend to maneuver a stroller inside. They walked past

Mauricio, close enough for him to see the baby inside the stroller, kept warm by a lime-green blanket. The girls beelined to the skinny window. The girl in the long skirt held her gaze the longest, the other already bored. "He looks so cute in pink," Mauricio heard the girl in the long skirt mutter. He wondered for a moment if she could be talking about Alonso, but something told him that he wouldn't go for a girl in a long skirt. Alonso wouldn't go for someone dutiful. He was smart enough to know why his parents had split up.

The girl with the baby took a quick look through the window. "What a dumb color," she said, and returned to fuss with the baby, who made little noises of contentment from her attention. It brought an involuntary smile to Mauricio's face—he could feel it form as he watched the girl tuck the lime-green blanket tighter around her baby. "Qué vida," he remembered Pico saying, after Pico had asked him if he liked having kids, "not that I'd ever want them myself." The girl happened to glance up at Mauricio and met his eyes with a flash that reminded him of how the young man with the oranges had looked at him. She turned her back to him. "Let's go," she said to her friend.

"They're almost finished," her friend said, her hand clutching at her long skirt. "I just want him to talk to me again."

"He's done with you," the stroller girl said. "Don't you get it?" She said it with such authority, such knowingness, and she pushed the stroller toward the lobby entrance so that her friend could see that she was serious. The girl in the long skirt turned to watch her go, clearly torn by the dancers not yet finishing and her friend already at the exit. She finally pulled herself away and followed her friend. Mauricio caught her eye briefly and was surprised to see her eyes welling up in tears. She seemed ashamed of herself and he wanted to tell her that there was nothing to regret for feeling however she was feeling. But it wasn't his place to do so. He wasn't her father.

When the dancing stopped, the teenagers started to file out. The girls all held the bells of their gowns as they made their way through the lobby, the boys wandering outside one by one, no one to answer to. Mauricio couldn't decide which of them had been the object of that girl's affection, which one could have been worth so much pining. All of the boys wore the same pink vest and bow tie, but the formality couldn't hide that this one was chubby, that one dull and bored looking. Alonso was last to step out. Scanning the lobby, he seemed surprised to see Mauricio there. Alonso fixed his eyes on him, trying to hide that he had been waiting for someone.

"Hey, Dad," he said. "What are you doing here?"

"Your mom sent me to pick you up."

"Oh, uh . . ." Now Alonso looked again at the bustle of the lobby, at the girls milling in and out of the bathroom, tied up in the drama of not getting their gowns dirty. "I was going to hang out with some friends, actually."

Mauricio lowered his voice a bit. "I know, but . . . right now, what your mom says, goes."

If Alonso had thought about protesting this, his face didn't show it. He started toward the lobby doors, not in any hurry, or with the impatient distance that he sometimes had when the entire family was together in public places. He kept pace with Mauricio, nodding his chin at a couple of friends who didn't stop to chat with him when they saw he was with his father now, and they made their way out to the parking lot.

Not too far away from the entrance, the two girls stood waiting, and when the girl in the long skirt spotted Alonso, Mauricio knew then that his son was the one she had been waiting for. Alonso didn't acknowledge her, but he quickened his pace to the car. Mauricio could tell that this was something he didn't want to share. It amazed him how transparent teenagers could be in their feelings. Everything was written in Alonso's suddenly hunched shoulders, as if he was trying to lower his height, make himself small and unnoticeable. It was so easy to detect. But wasn't it always so easy to spot someone pulled helplessly along by who they really were? He could still see the faces of Alba's chola sisters all those years ago, Giggles and La Troubles, sitting in the back of a Buick Skylark. The two older guys sitting up front. Mauricio had been unloading heavy boxes in front of the furniture store when the Skylark slowed down, as if the guys had wanted to give the girls a look at him, make him aware of just how big his arms had gotten from all the lifting. The chola sisters looked him over, their eyes telling him that all that muscle was wasted on a boy like him. The guys in the front seat of the Skylark laughed as they sped away. They left Mauricio standing with the weight of everything suddenly so overwhelming and sharp that he had to set his box down and wipe his brow. They saw through his look of deep concentration, of focusing on the job at hand, his single-mindedness. They detected his avoidance, his studied endurance nothing more than the look of someone with too much to bear.

In the car, Alonso moved the carnations from the passenger seat so he could sit, but once they were in his hand, he regarded them closely. "Who are these for?" he asked, hesitating, as if maybe he wondered for a moment if the flowers could be for someone besides his mother.

"Those . . ." Mauricio sighed. "Well, your mother doesn't really like carnations."

"Does this mean you're coming home?" Alonso blurted out.

Mauricio started the car, but other parents had arrived in the parking lot now, so they would have to wait their turn to get out. "One step at a time," Mauricio said. "Maybe," he said. "I don't know."

He turned to see if the girls were still hanging about and they were, slowly making their way to the opposite end of the parking lot, the girl in the long skirt looking directly at their car. It wasn't any of his business, but he was Alonso's father. "Is that your girlfriend?" he asked. "Why don't you give her those flowers?"

Alonso laughed. "Stupid shit," he said, and he sounded like what Mauricio imagined those two guys driving the Skylark would have sounded like, crude and ready to make fun of everything. But as Mauricio started to turn out of the lot, Alonso said, "Okay, yeah . . . let me," pointing at the girls, and Mauricio pulled over a bit to let the other cars pass. Alonso bounded out with the carnations in his hand and when he got to the girls, sure enough he offered them to the one in the long skirt. Whatever was between them, Mauricio could see it from across the distance of the parking lot, something innocent that he envied. If innocent was the word. What was the word for it? He rested both hands on the steering wheel, patient as he watched Alonso hand over the carnations, the girl in the long skirt reaching up to receive them, her face crumbling into joy. Compromiso, he thought. He remembered. What Pico said when he told him he was in love. "Impossible," Pico had said. "You can't fall in love with someone with too many obligations. A few, yes, because we all have some. But if you have too many, love is impossible."

Someone behind him honked impatiently but Mauricio waved them to go around. He was watching Alonso speak to the girl in the long skirt, nothing to hide anymore. It was so easy and clear to see, the way the two guys driving the Skylark had seen him, the way Giggles and La Troubles had laughed. The way Pico had spotted him at the counter of the Woolworth's from the moment he had walked in. The young woman in the Crest movie booth, handing over the tickets. The bartender at La Fiesta who always gave them a free round, no questions asked. The young man with the oranges, suddenly aware that he was being looked at. Alba at the door just a while ago, staring him plain in the face. Or Alba, really, from the very beginning, looking up from the delivery receipts and ignoring everything her chola sisters warned her about. How life could have been so different if he had been a little braver about what he was feeling. He felt for the girl pushing the stroller, bending down to her compromiso, then rising up again to see if the conversation had finished. Not yet. And so she nudged the stroller just a bit, back and forth, back and forth, waiting and waiting, though Mauricio understood it was already too late.

FIELDWORK

When I was younger, I dreamed aloud about leaving the Valley and my mother's question was always, To do what? She asked it in Spanish, of course, and the single answer—the only answer—I could have dared was trabajo. Work demanded everything of my family. My mother had come to the Valley from Texas when she was very young because of work. Her older sister had gone ahead of her for the same reason (though my mother later told me that my tía was all talk, that she never worked a day in her life). Her brothers—my tíos— hunched everywhere in the fields, no matter the season. The Valley was all about work if you wanted it and Fresno was a city big enough for anyone. My best friend told me that his family, like mine, had come to the Fresno area because of the fieldwork, too. His father and his mother drove a truck from town to town, looking for crops to pick, and they lived like that until the truck broke down on Highway 99 outside of Selma. They had no money to fix the truck, so they settled there.

My best friend doesn't know if this story is entirely true or not, but I can easily picture his father, cigarette in hand, standing at the

side of the highway and wasting no time making a decision. His father, like mine, is pragmatic, with little patience for dreaming. His
father, like mine, had come up from Mexico, the poorest of the poor,
just as many Mexican fathers had come before them. And here was
my father now: still not dreaming, but sleeping deeply in the fluores-
cent dullness of a county rehab center, recovering from a stroke, and
[*his dad*]
me, out of work, tasked by my mother to look after him.

We had been alternating overnights at the rehab center, my mother
and I, sleeping in my father's room and then switching off after the
morning meal. This vigilance was completely unnecessary, I thought,
but my mother had a fear that the nurse would be English-only.
They're trained for this, I told her in Spanish, embarrassed by our
constant presence, but near the end of the first few weeks with him,
I witnessed his alarm when a nurse awakened him in the middle of
the night for medications and a blood withdrawal. His disorienta-
tion was so strong that it could only have translated into pain. He
struggled to rise from the bed, as if he sensed that he was being kept
in the room against his will, and the English-speaking nurse had no
words to calm him. Tranquilo, tranquilo, I kept saying to him, but
my voice was nothing he recognized. He seized against both of us
for a good long while before the nurse tapped the call button and
someone came in to assist, drawing the curtain around the bed, and
leaving me to listen to him whimper quietly back into sleep.

[*treating his child like a stranger*]

After that, I stayed awake all through the unsettling quiet of
the dark hours, the hallways so still I was convinced that the night
nurses had left their posts. I leaned back in the uncomfortable armchair and stared up at the ceiling, wondered if my father could dis-
cern that his road would end here, in a county rehab center in the
Valley, thousands of miles from where he was born.

Dawn had hardly cracked when a nurse came in to check on my
father. I didn't recognize her but she regarded me with a steady, un-
fazed look that reminded me of the flat disinterest in the voices con-

stantly asking my father for his full name, the day of the week, the month, his birthday, if it rained yesterday.

And who are you? the nurse asked me, hardly rousing my father.

I'm his son, I answered, but the word didn't seem to be enough for her. I thought I heard a certainty in her voice, as if she already knew my story. She must have been coming in on the previous nights, when I had actually been asleep, and wondered about me slumped in the armchair. What did she want to hear? I could have told her anything, I realized, true or not. My father, born over there, and me, his son, born over here. And yet here we were, in a county rehab center. Would it matter more if I said a substitute teacher, the youngest brother, the one who had never gone to jail, a fieldworker at one time? Would it matter more if I told her I had kids of my own or no children at all? I'm his son, I repeated, maybe too sharply.

I didn't mean anything by it, said the nurse. She turned her full attention to my father, who had stirred awake, and checked his vitals. Good morning, she said to him. She smiled now, genuine, and encouraged my father to sit up in bed.

My mother is usually here with him for breakfast, I said.

Not you? she asked.

We alternate, I told her. Me and my mother.

That's good of you, the nurse said. You know, you don't have to be here all the time if you need to rest. Neither does your mother. It's okay to go home or go to work.

Work, my father said.

The nurse, like all the others, encouraged him to speak as much as possible. You think he should go back to work?

Yeah, my father said, awake now and ready to agree to anything.

What was your job?

He looked at me, maybe realizing that his single-word English had reached its limit.

You picked crops, right, Dad?

Yeah, he agreed, but with great hesitation, as if he had to think about it to be sure.

Really? remarked the nurse. She was preparing to draw a vial of blood from him and I could tell she welcomed his distraction.

Just like all the men who had gone up north to the Valley before him, I thought, and wired back money from picking oranges and grapes and peaches. Naranjas, right, Dad?

When he heard the Spanish, he nodded and continued recalling in his own language. Cotton and tomatoes, too. And almonds, my father added, and figs and nectarines, there was so much work. Apricots, plums, corn, pistachios, the lemon groves over on the eastern slope of the Valley into the Sierras. Walnuts and cauliflower. Cherries and pears. He kept remembering things. Strawberries hiding in the dirt. Pecans. Persimmons. Avocado trees in the prettiest green rows you've ever seen. Olives and wheat. Hay bundled up for the horses and the cows. Apples, because the Americans liked their pies.

You picked all those things? I asked him.

Yeah, my father said, nodding his head.

That's a lot of work, the nurse said. I didn't think that she actually knew Spanish, only that she learned how to hear the end of things. She finished up with my father and looked at me. If you help him at breakfast, see how much he can do on his own, okay? Someone will come in shortly and help him bathe and dress.

I nodded at her in thanks. The room had brightened with morning sun. The exhaustion of the sleepless night hit me and I leaned my head back, just for a moment.

There was so much work in the Valley, my father said, I thought you could get rich, the way people talked about it.

Then, after a moment, he recalled, unbidden, the first place he had ever lived in the Valley, a trailer parked illegally near a highway overpass. The owner would move it every few nights, in case the county sheriff came by.

Do you remember it? he asked me.

Yes, I lied. I wanted just a moment to nap before my mother came.

It's true, my father said, that he came to the Valley only because others had talked about it. If enough people had said go to Texas instead, he would've gone. Or if enough people had reported that good things could happen in Los Angeles, he would've gone. As long as word came back. As long as word reached him. It was his bad luck that he had never known anyone who could have told him about Denver or Chicago. Or New York City. New York City, he marveled. Imagínate . . .

He said the word with a mix of bitterness and regret that made me snap to attention, prepared to see him edge into agitation. Tranquilo—I had the word on the tip of my tongue, but he softened his voice when he said, Look at your mother.

his dads unhappy w/ his life choices

I thought she had entered the room, but he was beginning a new story. Look at your tía with eleven kids to feed and not enough work in Texas. Work that other people were too proud to do, even if their kids were hungry.

But when you came here, you didn't have mouths to feed, I told him.

He had his mother in Mexico and plenty of cousins, he told me, young ones who couldn't do for themselves.

Did I know, my father asked, the story of the man who had knocked on my mother's back door one Sunday morning because he had wound up in our little town on a bright hot summer day while the whole neighborhood was at church and so no one else had answered his knocking? The man was lost and he was hungry and he had nowhere to go and my mother—she wasn't a churchgoer—gave him two tacos wrapped in tinfoil and a drink from the garden hose, and she told him to let it run a bit so the hot rubbery taste could pass and the colder water could come through.

You're like your mother, he said. Before I could ask him how, he said, Everyone is a hungry child in the end.

He closed his eyes, tired already of the morning, though nothing of his day had begun, and when the next nurse came in, she had trouble getting him to focus on his task. You're getting a bath before breakfast, Dad, I told him, and I helped guide him to the bathroom.

The nurse eased him into his shower seat, talking him through every step, raising his arms to take off his shirt, then gently pulling them down when he continued reaching toward the ceiling. Slower, the nurse said, when my father tried to rush through the lowering of his sweatpants and his underwear, meek and naked now except for his socks and a pair of slippers.

Here, I'll do that. It was my mother, who had arrived so quietly that I couldn't tell how long she'd been watching from behind me, if she had seen my hesitation in helping. Whoever is going to do this at home, the nurses had said many times, should get used to doing this safely. My mother moved past me impatiently and bent down to remove my father's socks and slippers. I was taking up space, doing nothing. I eased myself out of the bathroom, listening to them attend to my father, hearing my mother hum in agreement as the nurse guided her, the simple, everyday task now one that couldn't be rushed.

In my father's quiet, in the dribble of water they used to bathe him, my mother would say Yes, yes to whatever the nurse was doing. They got the job done with unhurried efficiency, walking my father back to the bed in a thin robe and clean underwear. To make myself useful, I selected a T-shirt and sweatpants for him, his clothing loose and easy to get into, and my mother grabbed them from me with annoyance.

You should go home and rest, she told me. You look tired.

I debated whether or not I should tell her about the night's episode with my father, his confusion, his stunted tongue, his moaning, as if he had tried to fill the room with some kind of noise to kill the confusing silence. Now, getting ready for breakfast, he was quiet but bright-eyed, cooperative with the nurse as they finished dressing him. Once he was ready, the nurse left us and my mother didn't say anything as I followed them to the dining room.

He greeted his two fellow patients. The quieter one sat at the end of the table, staring off at the door, disconsolate as his breakfast ran cold, his wife yet to appear. He didn't want any of the nurses to help him, his eyes fixed on the door. The other man ate unassisted, his hands spry with the plastic utensils. Both of these men were my father's age. The nurses liked my father because of his improvement in speaking; the men could understand and respond in Spanish, an encouragement in their recoveries. They sometimes talked like the old Mexican men who gathered at our town bakery at six in the morning.

I leaned over to cut up the sausages on my father's tray. Let him do it, my mother said. He needs to practice.

My father was already trying to rope me into a conversation with his two fellow patients.

He wants to know, my father said—meaning me—why you—meaning the old man with the spry hands—came to the Valley.

I didn't have to say to my mother that I had never asked such a question. She knew how my father would say anything to start some chatter at breakfast, no matter who was at the table or what the subject might be.

The old man with the spry hands finished his breakfast and pushed his tray forward. He was thin, more on the gaunt side, and yet he cleaned his plate at every meal. He had come from Mexico as well, in the same long-ago years as my father, and he had found work at a dairy farm, feeding and caring for the cows. An older brother, who had gone up north before him, had told him to look for work in the dairies and he found the job easily, the first and only dairy he had ever approached.

In those days, my father said, you could find work anywhere. People these days don't want to work. Turning to me, he said, You see?

My mother looked at me as if to ask what had gotten my father so interested in work, but then the quiet man's wife came, flustered and panicked. Because there were no nurses around, she eyed my mother when she saw the full breakfast tray, as if it were her responsibility to feed him. My mother said buenos días to her anyway.

And you? my father asked, as the quiet man waited for his wife to cut up his pancakes.

Let him eat his breakfast in peace, my mother said. To my surprise, she reached over and picked up my father's coffee cup, helped him steady it to his lips.

Oranges, said the old man with the spry hands. Isn't that right, señora? Isn't that what your husband did for a living?

The quiet man's wife watched us, spooning a bit of egg to her husband, unsure about the question or why it was being asked. She had the look of someone who had been asked a lot of questions about work—if she had it, the kind she had, and for how long. If she had the necessary documents, if she understood how she would be paid. And she had the look of someone who knew better than to answer.

He picked oranges, said my father. ¿Te acuerdas? he urged the quiet man to remember.

You're from Ivanhoe, said the old man with the spry hands. You told us that you were from Ivanhoe. There's nothing but oranges over in Ivanhoe.

The whole east side, my father said. All those towns that are almost in the mountains. Orange Cove up north and Lemon Cove down south.

Citrus, said the old man with spry hands.

Grapefruit, said my father. I picked those before. Some as big as your head.

Mentiroso, my mother interrupted. You never picked grapefruit

in your life, she said. And then, to me, what have you been talking
to him about?

Work, I said. Then I thought of how I had never heard those
stories—not once, not at all—and I realized that maybe work
wasn't exactly what we had been talking about. My father; the man
with the spry hands who struggled to recover any use in his legs; the
quiet man who remained just as quiet through his pancakes: these
men who worked all their lives in the fields of the Valley, making
do with whatever the state could provide now that their bodies had
given out. But their minds hadn't. Their stories were not yet lost in
their heads.

memories are the most important part

You shouldn't believe everything he tells you, my mother said.

The quiet man's wife kept her attention on my mother as she fed
her husband. She glanced at me, too, surprised that a son was present to help in feeding. This was women's work.

Do you have other children besides him? she asked my mother.
She gestured with her head in my direction, as if I were not in the
room.

Yes, I do, my mother answered.

How many? asked the wife.

I thought my mother took too long to answer. But then she said,
I had six.

It was the truth, though it was not something I expect my mother
to say. I had always heard her say five. I thought of myself as the
youngest of five. Maybe it had to do with the way the woman was
cleaning her husband's chin, helping him hold a cup of coffee. Maybe
it had to do with knowing that my father, in his current state, would
try to correct a story if it wasn't the way he understood it. My mother
would keep the peace. But I knew a different story.

When I was fourteen, a teenager who didn't know any better, about
asking personal questions, about holding in pain, my mother told
me that, yes, it was true there had been a baby, the first one before

the others came, but I had to understand that this was never some-thing to ask a woman about, ever. It was none of a man's business. She was fourteen—the same age I was when I was asking her about this—when she had the baby. I was thinking about why my old-est siblings had been born in Texas and the rest of us in the Valley. I was young enough to believe that something bigger—fate, des-tiny, God's will—was responsible for my being born in a place like ours, one of the many dusty towns dotting the fields around Fresno. It could have been Yettem, my mother told me. Or Seville, even smaller places on the map, but she was long done with towns that didn't have hospitals. The baby had developed a fever and they drove to another town that had a hospital, the baby wrapped in a blanket. She didn't have the English to explain what was wrong with the baby and no one at the hospital spoke Spanish. This was in Texas, back in those years. They took the baby from her and she tried to follow them into another room, but they wouldn't let her. She could see through the glass in the door, though, and she watched them lift the baby from the blanket, strip it of its diaper, and place it in a tub of water. She heard the baby wail from the shock of the water and then the crying softened, as if the fever had broken, and then the baby made no more noise.

her first child died

The baby had pneumonia? I remember asking this, because back then I thought there should always be an answer to everything.

My mother responded that she didn't know English at the time. It was her way of saying that she had always wondered, but that she had no way of asking about something she had not been allowed to understand. It was something that she didn't want to be made to re-member, so there were five of us children, just five.

And yet here we were, so many years later, in front of strangers, with my mother saying six. A truth in front of people who wouldn't know any better and maybe wouldn't care. The wife continued feed-ing her husband some more and he ate as if in great thought. She kept her attention on my mother and then my father asked her ¿Y usted? Where was she from and why had she come to the Valley?

I knew the answer would be Mexico and I knew the answer would be she came because of her husband. I knew the answer would be there was no other choice but to come north. I listened with the respect my mother had taught me and I asked no questions when she said that picking oranges was a good and steady job. The Valley had been, she said, a good place to live. It had been hard work, but she didn't have any complaints.

I stayed quiet as my mother and this woman exchanged more pleasantries. They listened to each other. They seemed to know how to ask questions that let them tell just enough of who they were. They recognized in each other where they could be transparent and yet not reveal everything. They responded to each other's telling with all the phrases I knew to show someone you were listening. ¿A poco? No me digas. ¿O sí? ¿Pa' qué te digo? The men fell silent as the women finished feeding them and then my mother gave me the cue that the conversation was about to end. Bueno, pero el pasado ya pasó. All that had come had already passed and she rested her hands on the here and now of my father's unsteady arm.

We still had weeks of this ahead of us, my mother and I. I would have to speak to the front desk and convince them that my father wasn't ready to be released. We would have more overnight stays and I decided to let my mother believe that he slept quite peacefully through the late hours, his grip improving, his eyesight coming back from what he said were the silver clouds. I must have slumped in exhaustion just thinking about it. Go home, my mother urged. Get some rest.

I cleaned up my father's spot at the table as they wheeled him off to his morning therapy session. I drove home, the midmorning already hot, and though I was hungry, it was sleep I really needed. By the time I arrived at my apartment, I couldn't keep my eyes open.

The curtains were already drawn—I did nothing anymore in my apartment these days—and I collapsed on the couch, arm over my eyes. I tried to sleep, but it would not come easily. I could hear my father's Yeah, yeah, his only way to agree, his only way to communicate with the nurses that he understood what they wanted him to do. I kept my eyes closed, took note of my breathing, concentrated to make it softer, more patient, to think of a calming place. Río, I could imagine my father whisper, and I drifted into the story of the first time he ever crossed into the United States. I felt myself step right into a river crossing with him, the river running thin, a strip of muddy water no more than ankle deep, easy enough to keep your shoes in one hand to make your way to the other bank. The memory of his voice telling the story sent me deeper into slumber. No one would notice me slipping into the water, he said. Rolling my pant legs back down and strolling over to the cantinas just a street over from the bridge. If you timed it right, you could cross at dusk before the mosquitoes got bad or the snakes slithered out to feed, easy as can be, so easy. No one would ever look at you twice if you made your way to El Gallo de Oro or El Tururú and spent the whole night eating American hamburgers and drinking ron y cocas.

When I woke, it was late afternoon and I was drenched in sweat. I got up from the couch, hungry, but the refrigerator was empty except for a pack of hot dogs. I speared one on a fork and held it over the open flame of the stove, like my father would do, sticking it in a corn tortilla. It was simple, but enough. I showered and got ready to go back to the rehab center. This cycle could only end one way, I thought to myself, getting in the car. I was still shaking off the day's dreaming when I realized that my father had told that story about the river to me as a story of pleasure, a brief joy he had wanted me to remember.

At the rehab center, my parents had a visitor, a primo from my mom's side of the family. Other cousins and tías and tíos had stopped by in the past weeks, but not Primo. It's that I'm working too many shifts, Primo said, and I could see he was nervous about seeing my father, hands in his pockets, maybe a little relieved that he was alert and able to speak.

You have it good here, Primo said, picking up the snack of applesauce waiting alongside my father's latest batch of pills. What a life, when they bring you whatever you ask for. You should stay here forever!

The way they laughed about this, I wondered how much of a joke it really was.

Do you know the story, Primo asked me, of the time we were out working the plum trees one summer? All day, we could see those damn green migra planes flying over us. And if we couldn't see them, we could hear them. I knew it in my bones that they were going to try to round us up and we should've quit working then and there.

The farmers don't pay on Fridays, my father explained, but I already knew this, just like I knew I had heard this story somewhere, sometime, in some version or other.

Sure enough, when we broke for lunch, the green vans came from all sides and we all took off running deeper into the trees. Even your father. But for what? They had us surrounded and the farmer knew none of us had papers.

Pues ya sabes la canción, my father said.

The same old song, I said.

Except your father, said Primo, pointing a finger at him, your father had papers. He had every damn document those cabrones could ever want. And what did he do? He ran with the rest of us!

They laughed about this, even my mother, as if it had been the first time the story had ever been told, harder still when my father laughed loudest of all. I could see in Primo a relief that there was something to joke about, that there was something to carry away the weight of worry. Because the story was clear in my father's mind, his eyes grew wider at every detail swimming back into his memory.

Imagínate, my father said. Yo con papeles . . . ¡y me mandaron a la chingada!

They laughed and laughed, so much so that one of the nurses in the hallway leaned in to shut the open door of the room, so much so that my father's favorite nurse finally came to gently remind Primo that visiting hours were over.

This man never wanted to work, said Primo, squeezing my father's forearm to show that he was only joking. Now he sleeps like the rich.

My mother eyed me as Primo left. I can stay with him overnight, she said. You don't look rested.

You know, neither of us has to be here. The nurses know what they're doing.

It's not the nurses I'm worried about, she said.

He's been fine, I told her, but I think she knew that something had happened. I think she knew that my worry was growing. She turned on the television set to the telenovelas, one of the sweeter romances of the early evening before the darker story lines hit the late hours.

She and my father watched a bit of it together, commenting on it as I watched silently alongside. She bid us goodnight as the credits rolled and before the next one began. My father watched uninterrupted, as if Primo had never been there at all, as if he and my mother hadn't just had a moment alone, even with me in the room.

And then—

We were like a bunch of birds when you step toward them too fast, you know what I mean? We all ran at the same time. Away from the road, breaking against the rows and trying to separate. You could see a migra van at the end of one row and try to run into the next. Funny how you can make out the green of a migra van through all those leaves.

Did they really deport you?

All the time, he said.

That time, I said. When you had papers and everything.

Yeah, my father said. Papers don't mean anything.

Did they listen to you when you told them you had papers?

On the television, a suitcase full of money was clicked open and two detectives glared at the man who had been holding it.

Dad, you did tell them, right?

He laughed. You think anybody ever believed me? You think people believe you just because you say something? You think all you have to do is say you have papers? Here, my father said, thrusting his hands out as if in offering. Here, my papers.

a his dad's secret [handwritten marginalia]

At eleven, the night nurse made him turn off the television, a full hour after he was supposed to. I dozed in the corner armchair, and I fell into a fitful sleep that soon had me running through an orchard, the trees with wide spaces between them, so much ground to cover so fast, the green leaves lush. They shimmered in that way that trees do when a breeze passes through them, the gentle rustle an awful warning, and I kept running, exhausted, expecting the branches to part and reveal an officer, a green van. Nothing came and the orchards yawned even wider. It occurred to me to stop running and start climbing, to go up, not out, and I lifted, floated into the trees, through the branches, and up above into the blue, blue sky.

when field work? romanticizing field work? [handwritten marginalia]

I woke with a deep sadness, the gray light of dawn seeping through the windows. I looked over at my father's chest, the bare rise and fall. He was still with me.

Are you afraid? he asked me.

Startled, I sat up. Are you okay, Dad?

I asked you a question.

No, I said.

I think you are, he said.

No, I replied.

Sometimes it's okay to be afraid.

I'm not afraid, I said, though I was, and I knew that speaking anything aloud to him would be nothing he could comprehend.

When those migra vans came, I ran, but I wasn't afraid. I ran because everyone else was running. You do what everyone else is doing. ¿Me entiendes?

He stayed quiet, the dawn light somewhere between a deep blue and violet, the shadows not breaking, and for a moment I did have a fear, that when the sun came in full brightness, my father wouldn't be there at all.

It's okay to be afraid, my father said. Right now, I'm afraid.

I had never known my father to be afraid, to be a fearful man, and I told him so.

Just one other time, he said. Just once, many years ago, when he was deported for the first time. He had been trucked somewhere in Arizona, or maybe it was El Paso, it was so long ago, but it was the desert and he knew the border was close by. He waited to be driven across and he was thinking of a river, because to cross over meant to cross a river. Instead, they were marched over to a wide expanse of cement that he realized was an airfield, and a transport plane, military green, waited with its engines running and a little ramp for them to climb aboard. All of them were young men and none of them had ever been on a plane before. They sat on thin benches that stretched along the sides and the two men in the cockpit told them that they should hang on if they knew what was good for them.

You've never been to jail, my father told me. You were too much of a good boy for that, but your brothers would know. Your brothers would know the insides of walls like that, what people carved in there because they wanted someone to remember them. That was the inside of that plane, just the benches and the metal walls. I read those terrible things and I thought they were going to throw us out of that plane.

But they didn't, I said.

Pues claro, he said.

After a pause, he asked me if I was a fearful person.

I don't think so, I told him.

Just like your mother. He was quiet again for a long time before I realized he had fallen back asleep.

Later, when my mother arrived, I was trying to help the morning nurse with my father's bath. My mother inserted herself in between us, motioning me to get out of the bathroom. I took out a clean set of clothes for my father and noticed my hands were jittery. I could only imagine how tired my eyes looked.

She and the nurse brought my father out in his bathrobe. No te ahogas en un vaso de agua, she said to me, with a slight huff. Don't drown in a glass of water.

I could feel the tiredness deep in my bones but I joined my mother in the dining room. She cut up my father's food, brisk and impatient, and I knew better than to say anything about how he should do it himself. The quiet man waited for his hurried wife and she came in eventually. The man with the spry hands continued his healing without a family member to help him. I nudged my father's coffee cup toward him. He held it with both hands, took a grateful sip, and greeted his two friends, life going on another day.

The quiet man's wife finished feeding her husband. What's your work? she asked and it took a moment before I realized she was addressing me.

No work, my father said, in English, as if I could only hear it that way. No work right now.

He wasn't wrong. My mother stayed silent, too, and if I wanted to take pride in who I was, I would have to answer for myself. But what did it matter who I was to a stranger? Who else did I need to be besides his son?

This time, it was my mother who cleaned up my father's spot at the table and the quiet man's wife did the same. The man with the spry hands wiped down his own. I expected my mother to urge me to go home, but she didn't say anything when I followed the group to the therapy room, where my father crowed at the sight of a young blond woman in pink scrubs.

La canadiensa, my father said, as if announcing her. We moved up to her work table.

Are you going to introduce me? the Canadian therapist asked cheerfully. I could see that she knew exactly how to work my father's attempted charm into an immediate test of his recall and response. She raised her hand at me almost imperceptibly when I started to answer for him. Who is he? she asked.

In the long moment before my father responded, the word stuck in my throat. My impatience to answer something so obvious was more about me than about my father's confusion. He had so much to come back from, rehabbing in English.

My son, he said finally.

That was going to be my guess, said the Canadian therapist. She placed an unplugged telephone on the table. Here, she said, pointing at the phone. Can you show me how to dial for help?

La canadiensa, my father said, pointing her to me. My son, he said, pointing to her, joking and smiling, trying to hide that he didn't know what to do with the strange object in front of him.

The Canadian therapist set up tasks for the three men. Here, she said, giving one of them a little red bowl of water and a dry washcloth. Can you show me how to clean your elbows?

She gave them sweaters with big colorful buttons. A door handle with a lock that had to be turned to open. A plastic medicine bottle with a twist top. A bare toothbrush and the paste still in the tube. A single shoe with untied laces.

My father struggled with the washcloth, unable to wring out the water. He's looking for the soap, I tried. That's why it's confusing him.

She shook her head at me and I knew I had broken the rule of not interrupting. Everything had to be learned again and only they could do it themselves. The Canadian therapist wrote down check marks on a piece of paper of all the things my father couldn't do on his own. I'm glad, she said, that he has family to help him through this. Not everyone does.

For the rest of the therapy hour, I waited with my mother at the side of the room. I put my head in my hands, leaning over in the chair, and this time I did want her to urge me to go home. I wanted her permission to leave.

What's wrong now? she asked.

Imagínate, I said to her, the lack of good sleep overtaking me, to be so broken after all that hard work, and to end up like this. How do they keep going?

All work is hard, my mother said. We all work in our own ways. Her eyes glimmered for just a flash. Mira esta, she said, so I could remember the canadiensa, the therapist who had come from so far away. She was telling me to look, but she was also reminding me to listen, to not stay in my own questions. Maybe I would hear what I needed to hear.

I tied vines one year, my mother said, when the money was low. I was pregnant with you, about seven months, but there I was. It must have been seven months because you were born in March and tying is January work, in the cold and the rain. You know what tying is?

I nodded yes. I had done it before.

She remembered, yes, because it's easy work for kids, for women untangling the vines like unruly hair, pruning them back a little, and then wrapping them back tight around the wires, the rows tidy and ready for the hotter months. It was still hard work, my mother said, all that mud and cold, and you just two months away from being born.

We watched my father as he negotiated a walker across the room, careful step by careful step. The old man with spry hands practiced stretching his upper arms and the quiet man was tasked with buttoning a shirt.

They'll get out soon if they do their exercises, my mother said, as if to remind me that this place was not the end. No place is the end if you don't want it to be. If you work hard, you can leave.

We watched my father quietly and I knew not to say a word. Seven months, my mother sighed, lost in thought. And then, a moment later, Men don't know how to suffer.

THAT PINK HOUSE AT THE END OF THE STREET ON THE OTHER SIDE OF TOWN

I.

Silvio, whom everyone called El Sapo, had been coming the longest, but only during the wet times when the fields ran muddy and no one else would brave the kind of cold that would lock your knuckles, no matter how thick the gloves. By spring, he'd return to a pueblito called Pozos, which made everyone ask why he'd go back to a hole in the ground. A frog crawling under the mud to wait out the heat. That was El Sapo, leaving sometime in early April before the heat came. And then the others would arrive. Fidelio and his twin brother Modesto who, for some reason, was several inches shorter than him. Jerónimo, quiet and stark, who claimed to know Silvio, but nobody knew for sure. Baldomero El Mero Mero, who boasted that he was the one who had shown the others how to start with a bus in Celaya, take it to the outskirts of Tijuana, and, right over there, at a llantería owned by his old friend Raimundo, you could sneak through the dust yard of Raimundo's old tires and cross to the other side, get to the highway on foot, and, if you were smart enough to hide your money, catch a Greyhound to a place called Goshen, where you'd go to the phone booth outside of the station, look out at the cotton fields as you dialed a number and told a man named Poldo that you'd made it across. A cousin by way of another cousin. A friend of the family. From Celaya. From Ojo de Agua. From La Cuevita. From Charco Blanco. Yes, yes, of course. A third yes if you promised you had the money to pay a little rent for a month. That's how Eliseo showed up. And poor Casimiro, who wore thick glasses and peered into the fruit trees with his whole face to see what he was picking. But you'd have to know Spanish to know why all the other men laughed at his name.

II.

Poldo was Leopoldo Ruelas, as thin as his mustache, who came out of nowhere and bought that pink house at the end of the street on the other side of town. That house had stood empty for a long time, the paint chipped and the weeds growing high and the bank only sometimes coming to clean up the yard. Not often because it wasn't a town where just anybody could buy a house. People rented and maybe they passed by the faded pink house with the enclosed back porch and wished that they could one day be its owner. Poldo had to be born here to do that. Mexicano, of course, but he knew how to get the kind of money to get a bank to talk to you, and he had a pretty wife who was taller than him, Belén, who led a toddler by one arm and cradled a baby with the other, and maybe it was she who decided to paint the house pink again. That was one reason why people thought she was from Mexico. If you bothered to dream about a house, only a true Mexican would dream about a pink one or one that was bright orange, up on a hill somewhere, looking down at everything else in drab colors, or worse, unpainted wood. Belén, who always wore dresses and high heels and knew just the store in Fresno where you could get a good deal on clothing de buenas marcas. Her little ones not yet old enough for anyone to know their names, but one looked like her and the other already with Poldo's rat face. Whether she was from over here or over there, Belén was the kind of person who had long ago stopped thinking about those days in some pueblito where you hoped into a little luck with a piglet given by a generous neighbor. She had dresses now and a family, a husband who could walk into a bank. She didn't have to sit around wondering if she should butcher the piglet or fatten it up, feed it the scraps or save them for herself. The hunger now or the hunger later.

III.

Poldo's truck left one morning and was gone for about an hour, which was just about time for the ida y vuelta to the bus station in Goshen, the one that sat out by the edge of a cotton field. He came back with one person. That's how Eliseo showed up. And just in time, too, because it was May and the fruit was coming in early. Poldo needed every hand he could get. Things were too busy to ask too many questions about why Eliseo had come up all alone or about exactly how he knew El Sapo or where he got all the money that he kept pulling out of his socks, the left front pocket of his brand-new Wrangler jeans, the shirt pocket of his long-sleeve. He wouldn't last more than a week in the fields, some of them said. Too slender, too quiet, and drinking only one can of beer. When he showed up, that made at least seven men from the other side sleeping on the enclosed back porch of the pink house at the end of that street. He wouldn't last, some of them said. He'd miss his mother too much. And with a name like that—too sweet for a full-grown man—you knew something bad was bound to happen to him.

IV.

The only one who ever made enough money to keep was Poldo. He hit them up for every dollar and he asked when they couldn't say no. At the Goshen bus station. For space on the back porch to sleep at night. A Saturday-night collection to buy carne asada and tortillas and beer. A Sunday collection for a sack of beans to last the week. For a ride out to the fields in the back of the truck. For the favor of having Belén stand in line at the Western Union office to send money home and coming back with the receipt. Sometimes a few dollars interest for having loaned out a week's pay to get started: you needed your own cutting knife, your own gloves, your own wide-brim, your own cazo y costal. Another pair of pants, work shirts, a fresh pack of underwear. Everyone with the same calcetines blancos hanging from the clotheslines. Just a few dollars more from everyone for a white bucket of detergent, a bottle of bleach. The washing machine outside by the toolshed sat idle all weekend, but you could slip Belén a few dollars and she'd have your clothes clean and folded on the back porch by sundown's return from the fields. And for the ones who couldn't always bear so much of the men's laughter in the backyard and the bored exhaustion around sundown, Poldo left them with just enough in their pockets for niceties like a bottle of Tres Flores or Lucky Tiger or English Leather, something to put on for an evening walk into town and a beer at John Henry's. Just enough for a few last coins to drop in the jukebox, a baile or two with a woman kind enough to say yes, but who wished she was someplace else.

V.

Of course Eliseo got hurt, but that wasn't the terrible thing. That would happen later. First came a stumble from the ladder in the nectarine orchard. Not from the very top, gracias a dios, but from the third or fourth rung, high enough to make an ankle spear through with pain, the knee swelling by nightfall. You work through that kind of hurt, just as you do when the cuchillo catches the soft valley between the thumb and forefinger, or your back seizes so much from stretching for high branches that no one makes you go up the ladder in the first place. They didn't send Eliseo back to the house right away. He waited by the side of the road until sundown while the rest of the men finished and Poldo docked his pay right down to the minute. If Eliseo had known any better, he would've asked for how much fruit had been weighed by twelve thirty in the afternoon, when he had to quit, and taken his share of that, rather than after the whole day, the men slower by the hour. In the backyard of the pink house that night, the rest of the men put him to ladling out the beans and heating the tortillas, knowing Eliseo wouldn't be rising at dawn to join them. They left it to him to rinse out the tin plates by the spigot next to the washing machine. If he was so weak-boned, if he was so frail, how would he last through the summer? No one had ever gone back early after going through so much to get here. So they kidded him all through the dishwashing and then later when they lay on the floorboards of the back porch and talked themselves to sleep. Then they rose at dawn quieter than usual, all of them, and left the blankets and pillows strewn around for Eliseo to fold. He could do women's work then, some of them said, as they rode into the dawn. He could put himself to good use.

VI.

No one told Poldo that they left Eliseo behind, and Poldo certainly wasn't the type to ask after anyone. You cared for yourself, showed up for your work, and that was that. Poldo wasn't one to assign rows or pair up the twins or separate fighters. You got the rows you got and, at the end of the day, Poldo did the math and split up the dividends. He could get sixteen rows by lunchtime if everyone worked like they were supposed to. So why had the men weighed in so little, what was wrong with the fruit? Poldo figured it out by lunchtime, no one saying anything to him once he had that look on his face. It clouded over with a jealousy none of them had ever seen before. His face wouldn't have looked like that had it been Sapo or Baldomero El Mero Mero. Or even if had been Modesto, the shorter of the twins, who had the odd, striking gray eyes of an animal, another difference from his brother. All the men went back into the trees to finish the day and they all, in their own way, could now imagine the slender Eliseo washing the tin plates under the outside spigot and then setting them aside to dry, Belén watching him from the open door of the back porch, the baby in her arms, the other child standing at her side, fingers in his mouth, fingers pulling at the hem of her dress.

VII.

A brother, a nephew, a primo. Too young to be anyone's tío and certainly not her son. Who was the stranger with Belén in town, limping alongside her, slender and slight? Why wasn't he out in the field like all the other men who worked for Poldo? Who paid for the plates they shared at the P&A diner, this man who was very mindful with her two children, like they were his or something? No . . . to even suggest such a thing. Maybe he had children of his own back in his pueblito. Maybe that's why he knew how to be so tender. But then again, some men know how to turn on affection when they need to. What was he trying to get, sitting at the P&A diner and finishing the lunch special like they had nowhere to go? The restaurant's swamp cooler made it hard to hear anything they were saying. They shared the table at one of the front tall windows, streaked and greasy. The older child left handprints all over it but Belén didn't bother to correct him too much. With a napkin in her beautiful hands, she absently swiped at the fingerprints on the glass, her red nail polish even brighter in the glint of afternoon light. She was too busy listening to whatever this stranger was saying. No, he wasn't a close friend of El Sapo. He wasn't a primo of Baldomero El Mero Mero. Everyone knew who he wasn't, but they didn't know who he was. Not even the name of the pueblito that he came from. No one knew anything for sure, except that something would surely change once Poldo found out.

VIII.

Had it been only men at the pink house, who would've minded if someone had brought back a woman from John Henry's? Who would've said anything if one of them waited until after dark and tucked themselves into the dark side yard, a narrow sliver between the house and a wooden fence? They could have laughed about it if the woman's moans carried through the yard, or snickered at their friend's grunting, prepped their jokes for how short it lasted. But it had been an unspoken understanding among all the men, whether they had been coming to the pink house for a long time or only once or twice, that they were never to bring women home. They should never disrespect Belén. They held their cursing around her. They kept their joking to gentle politeness and left their dirtiest jokes to the cackling whispers on the back porch, out of earshot.

That night, after Eliseo had stayed at the house and Poldo had figured out that he was a man short on the crew, the men felt a thickness settle over the backyard, where they were drinking the day's work away. A heated conversation began to carry over all the way past the back porch. Belén's voice was short and quick, pausing here and there, as if she were thinking about what to say. Poldo grew louder as he questioned her. The men couldn't ignore it and it made a few of them realize what little regard they had given to their own privacy. No place to take a woman if they wanted some time with her. The cramped bathroom off the back porch, where at least the noisy water heater hid the rudest sounds. The sounds of the first hacking coughs at dawn, impossible to sleep past once it started. But those were all things they could ignore if they wanted to. Not so with Poldo's questions getting louder, sterner, then shouting over Belén. And then, of course, the two little children started to cry, a terrible sound that the men didn't know what to do about because it was always their sisters, their primas, their mothers and grandmothers who quieted down that need.

But not this time. The children kept crying, Poldo kept shouting, and they realized they couldn't hear Belén anymore. After a time, not even Poldo. Just the children with their endless tears and not one of them moved to check on them until Eliseo, of all people, started walking toward the pink house from the dark backyard. Let him, one of them whispered to the others, so Poldo could deliver what was coming to him.

Moments later, the children had calmed and Eliseo came back out, leading one by the hand, the other in the crook of his arms. They could hear him whispering to them, small hiccups from the little boy as if he would start all over again. The little boy looked out into the dark backyard at the men gathered there, looking back at him.

From inside the house, finally, some faint movement, and then the men saw Belén's figure move onto the porch. She'd returned from wherever she'd disappeared. She took the children from Eliseo. Even with everyone quiet, they couldn't quite hear what she said to him. They couldn't even tell if he nodded at her, only that she took the children back into the house.

IX.

Lo que pasó, pasó en un jueves. A Thursday at the end of May, the worst day of any month. The next day, sometimes people wouldn't get paid, empty promises for cash on Monday first thing, or foremen long gone and hard to find. Or the green migra vans would start to circle around, always passing the work trucks at dawn as if they had so many roundups that they couldn't be bothered checking out a small group of six or seven men. Thursdays were the last full days of work, bringing a dread that left some of the older men who'd seen things quieter and solemn when they rose at dawn and here, finally, the younger respected what their elders might know.

That Thursday, right at dawn, they woke one by one to the sound of sobbing. Some of them had been so deep in sleep that they'd let themselves dream of someone from back home, haunted now by their pleading. Some huerca, some cualquiera, the sooner they left Celaya or Ojo de Agua the better. Who needed the hassle of love like that? But in their dreams, some of the men felt their wrong for the first time. When they opened their eyes, thinking they were the first ones awake, they lay there watching the dawn start to slowly light the back porch, the huddled forms of the other men still fast asleep, and they promised themselves a way to ask forgiveness. Lo siento, one of them thought, how wrong it was to leave someone in tears, to not let their sorrow ever pierce them. Confession on Sunday morning, another promised himself, his dead mother's voice counting back to him the fruits of the spirit: amor, gozo, paz, benignidad, her voice said to him. Bondad, fe . . . but then the sobbing started again, not a dream after all. Poldo's stern voice, low and mean, and answered only by the sobbing.

The men rose. They tidied up the coarse blankets and sheets that served as their back-porch pallets. Someone heated beans on last night's resurrected ashes, preparing everyone's taco lunches in tinfoil in the backyard because they knew they wouldn't be going into the kitchen this morning. They showered quickly enough that everyone actually got hot water, got themselves into clean work clothes. They went about their morning pretending not to hear the sobbing turn into more anguished cries, not to hear the sickening thud of flesh being hit, slapped, something falling over. Then silence. Not even the children made a sound. ¿Me entiendes? they heard Poldo say, his voice as imposing as a church bell in the morning air. They waited by the work truck before two more brutal golpes landed on flesh. Fuerte, fuerte, a sound some of them recognized, deeply ashamed of themselves for those times when they'd hit women in their families, or when they had watched it happen but said nothing at all.

Poldo came out and he didn't have to say a word about Eliseo loading up on the truck with the rest of them, hurt ankle or not. They piled into the back, hurrying as Poldo revved the engine and sped off before some of them had even gotten in. Later, some would say that Eliseo was in tears. Later, some would say that they had looked back at the pink house and they had glimpsed Belén on the doorstep. Bien sangrada, because that was the only way to describe the condition of her face, the mix of tears and blood and bruising.

Poldo took them out to the orchard where it was business as always. You two go here. You over there. Counting ahead down the orchard lines to see how many rows they could get in by noon or if they'd have to go see another farmer. They'd get paid, though. Poldo always came through. He wasn't afraid to harass the white farmers. He wasn't afraid to get out what his men had put in. They set to work, all of them except Eliseo. Poldo had given him no direction and he waited by the truck bed, knowing better than to ask. He had a hurt ankle, of course. But some of them had thought for sure that Poldo would've punished him with the hard work of climbing the ladders, hauling the heavy costales back for weighing. ¿Te creés muy chingón? A ver quien es pinche hombre, cabrón.

But who were they to tell Poldo the right way to punish a rival? Who were they to tell Poldo why he made such a big mitote out of a guy no one really knew? Who were they to tell Poldo that Eliseo was probably a joto anyway and sometimes women went for the soft types? They were there to work and they climbed the ladders and yanked the fruit, slipping into the dark morning heat of the orchards, Eliseo remaining at the truck bed all the while. The sun rose higher and the morning lengthened into its bright, relentless light. That's when it happened, the bad thing. They were all deep in the orchard, far away from the road, but still close enough to see the shape of one of those green migra vans, its bright gold star winking at them from the road. They saw two officers come out, bulky and towering over Eliseo, more slender than ever. They watched like rabbits in the field, statue-still, resisting the urge to run, the two officers putting Eliseo's arms behind his back and leading him to the van. And they remained like that, afraid to move, but thinking maybe they should, the officers no doubt returning. But no. It was only Eliseo that they took, the green migra van's taillights lighting up as it shifted to drive away.

X.

And that was how Eliseo disappeared and no one ever saw him again, said Modesto, the shorter of the twins, who liked to tell the story first anytime someone new entered the fold.

And that's how everyone knew Eliseo wasn't anyone's primo or anyone's friend, said Fidelio. Because no one ever missed him. No one ever called looking.

And that's why he needed to know family connections, Baldomero El Mero Mero said, before he told you how to get from Celaya to Mundo Llantería, because his friend Raimundo wasn't just going to let anyone slip through his tire yard anymore.

But that's what you should expect when you step out on the town with another man's wife, said one of the women at John Henry's, because she was sick and tired of women always taking the blame in stories like that. Love is already hard enough.

But Belén had never been satisfied with the good life she had, her sister said. Always looking for something better when she had a man's man right under her damn nose. It had to be her who called the migra. It had to be. Someone had to call if they came to pick up only one person. Because normally they'd go after everybody. They'd chase everybody down in the field until they caught every damn one. So no. Someone called just for him. Belén did. It was either him or get another bunch of cachetadas. But that's Belén. Saving herself so she could go on living in that ugly pink house. Lookit, her sister says, whenever she tells the story, tugging at her souvenir PISMO BEACH T-shirt that Belén had given her. Everything pinche pink.

But that's not how people should ever treat each other, said Casimiro, many years later, when he could barely see anymore, but had fallen into the good luck of meeting a woman named Raquelita. They had married, too late to have a baby, but they had each other. They traded stories of people they had known, family they still had, the cartas that went back to Mexico. The morning visita that came every once in a while, friends of theirs because they believed in being good neighbors. That's when the stories happened. That's when they remembered so and so and that and then. Pobrecito, Casimiro said, when they told this whole thing, and the air settled sad on the front porch where they were sitting. What a terrible thing for no one to ever hear from you again. Not family. Not friends. ¿Y Belén? Who knows? But she finally left one day, the kids too, and Poldo sold the house. That house at the end of the street? It used to be pink, if you can believe it. Toda sangrada, Raquelita shuddered, though she had not witnessed it, only heard Casimiro tell the story of Belén being thrashed like that. Pobrecita.

Out on the front porch, telling stories through the morning with whoever the visita might be. The noon hour would climb closer and they brought out the portable radio and the newsprint bingo cards from the Table Supply market. El color es verde, the announcer on Radio Bilingüe declared, reminding the players of the color of card

they needed to play to win. The announcer called out the numbers and Casimiro squinted at his cards, falling behind. Raquelita
helped him when she could. He could spot the letters at the top of
the grid, but the numbers were a jumble. No le hace, he said. They
played with dry beans as markers, listening to the numbers, a chance
to get away from the weight of the day, of whatever story had risen
that morning. Qué vida, Casimiro sighed, lucky to have Raquelita's
patient fingers pointing him toward the right numbers. He felt reas-
sured, though for a moment, sometimes just looking at Raquelita's
hands—anyone's hands—made him think of Poldo's hands, his fists.
Such cruelty and ugliness. Pobres, he thought again, and thought of
his own hands, his last shaky reach into the trees when he knew he
couldn't work anymore. The last golden peach he'd ever pick. Pobres,
he thought again, waiting through the quiet for the next number, but
his mind couldn't help but picture Belén's beautiful hands reaching
for a black telephone, the bright red nail polish, her finger in the rotary dial for the operator. Pobres.

WHAT KIND OF FOOL AM I?

I lied to myself all my life. To my mother and father, less so. But that was only because my father rarely spoke and my mother hardly listened. I didn't lie often, but I lied about what mattered. It fell on me to explain my little brother to them, why Teo did the things that he did. He wasn't a terrible child by any stretch, but he was stubborn and had to be told twice about everything. I had the notion that I would have no such allowances, and that any punishment inflicted on Teo would come doubly so for me. One time, when we were very young, we tailed our mother at the five-and-dime as she lingered among the fabrics. We played among the draped displays, pulling cloth across our faces like bridal veils, until our mother shooed us away, worried that we would dirty or tear what she couldn't afford. In the cosmetics section, while our mother was preoccupied with the saleslady ringing up her purchase, I watched Teo pocket something. He did it quickly, I remember, and I had the sense that he hadn't even really considered what he had taken. He guarded his treasure with a fist in his pocket so deep that he looked like he needed to pee. At the front counter, the clerk kept glancing at him in alarm, rushing our mother's purchase. I was sure the clerk had found him out, so I drew Teo in, shielding him from my mother, and yanked the small plastic case from his pocket. I gave him a look that he seemed to understand. He kept quiet, even when our mother startled us both by slapping me in front of the clerk before placing the case on the front counter. It was eye shadow, I would learn later, when I studied the clutter of my mother's dresser and learned the names for things, sometimes with Teo at my side, sometimes in a mood that was all my own.

This was in a little town called Mathis, Texas, and I was twelve when I first started to realize that I lived in a place that wasn't ever going to change much. Now and then, our father would drive the family to Corpus Christi to shop at Woolworth's or to sit in the orange plastic chairs of some state services office. The trip was only thirty minutes or so but I could feel the air change, thicker and saltier, and the city seemed to get busier every time I saw it. Our father must have sensed my thrill at seeing the blue-green line of the Gulf horizon and after errands he would loop by the bay so we could point at the sail-boats bobbing or gaze up at the rib cage of the bridge arcing us across the harbor. I had no deep imagination then about the water. It was only an end point, a place that stopped you and showed that there was no choice but to turn back to the sun-white streets of Mathis. So lost was I whenever I saw the Gulf that I failed to notice that my brother was quiet, too, and searching in his own way.

Teo must have been planning his someday even then. Where I took note of the wide Gulf and the tall buildings on the water's edge, he must have been seeing the nightclub fronts shuttered against the daylight, the neon signs hungry for dark. We'd pass those places from one end of the city to the bay and I noticed my father's atten-tion on the road, my mother just as stern. This was always where I would start looking for Teo, years later when he was sixteen and his impatience ran him away.

The lying had started in small ways: how it was the teachers who just didn't like him or how the principal had it out for the brown kids, especially the boys. I knew deep down that my parents didn't believe me, but I thought it was my duty to protect my little brother. Teo was restless in school, sneaking out of class, snapping at the teachers in a new and sullen voice that startled me when I first heard it. His voice deepened as he grew taller and thinner, but it was a mean sound, hardened by his restlessness. I got the sense, at times, that Teo hated me. Not for sticking up for him, but for not dreaming like he did, for not wanting any more for myself.

The first time Teo didn't come home, it was my mother who broke the quiet in the house after the sun had long since gone down. She kept peering out of the window, alert to some phantom noise on the street. This was May, near the end of my senior year, and we had been allowed to go to backyard barbecues and the last dance at the high school. I knew without asking that I was to be home before dark and even Teo didn't break that rule at first. This freedom was a kind of test, I knew, and I stayed within bounds, not knowing what life was going to be like once school ended. We went to bed that night with the kitchen light on and I could hear my mother rising every now and again to look out on the street. I didn't share her worry that something terrible had happened to my brother. I knew that he had simply gone away and I lay in bed in a kind of awe about his arrogance. Had it been me, I would have come home late once or twice, watching the sun give way to dusk, getting home when the orange had faded out, the stars only beginning. He knew he wouldn't be punished and this realization grew my resolve to make him come back home. As much as I understood that he had run away to something new, the unfairness of his being able to do so kept me awake until nearly dawn. When I got up the next morning, earlier than usual, I told the first big lie to my mother. "I know where he is," I said, "but he won't come home if we all go get him."

How many lies did I tell when I said that? I was only guessing that he had gone to Corpus. But it worked. My father set the keys to his Chevy truck on the kitchen table without a word and I knew not to rush away just yet. We calmly ate a breakfast of beans and potatoes and coffee and, at ten on the dot, I walked out to the truck as if I had been sent on the simplest errand. I held my breath as I stepped off the porch, already picturing someone in town seeing me behind the wheel of my father's truck, turning not to my tía's house, but onto the road that led out of Mathis. Yet I was deliberate, focused. I watched as I shifted the gear over to the orange R on the dash and it was only then that I noticed the small mercy of a full gas tank. I would have to think of every step, I told myself, and not rely on luck.

I drove out on the highway with a strange alertness, a sense of destination and release. I had never left town alone and even the fields felt new to me, not dusty or muddy, but dotted through with the green of the coming crop. They held a promise that I thought Teo was foolish to refuse. He wanted more though and when I drove into the heart of Corpus, it wasn't the Gulf air or the bustle that caught my attention. I could see now that it was a grimy city, salt-coated and open too wide to the white heat of the coming summer. I drove past the pool halls and the cocktail lounges promising Girls! just inside their dark hallways. Outside of one of the bars, a man lay drunk in the sun, his chin slack and his feet bare, but the streets were too empty. No one noticed him, just as no one would notice a sixteen-year-old boy wandering one day and then not there the next.

At the edge of the bay, I spotted Teo sitting near one of the long walkways jutting out into the water. I knew his frame anywhere and he looked even thinner and smaller because of the man next to him. I could see they were eating, a greasy bag between them, Teo taking quick, greedy bites. He didn't notice me in our father's Chevy truck. He'd nod at something the man was saying, but I could tell even from far away that he was only agreeing with whatever the man wanted.

"Teddy, who's she?" I heard the man say, when I approached the walkway and Teo had finally noticed enough to wave as if he had been expecting me all along. The man was as old as our father, paunchier but well dressed, his balding hair cut close on the side, more glimmers of pepper than salt. The closer I got to them, the more the man's face changed, crumpling over to a kind of alarm. It made it easier to speak when I saw him do that, to be the one who answered his question.

"I'm his sister," I said. "I came to take him home."

"We were just having burgers is all," the man said and he half-shoved the bag over to Teo. How easy to spot a lie, I thought, and I realized something about my parents. They could sense the truth behind my hesitations, a soberness in my voice going high, whatever it was I wanted to hide. Worse yet, I knew immediately that the man's lie was hiding something I had interrupted, something shameful. I was sure of what I had to say.

"He's only sixteen," I said, and the man turned to Teo with a stricken expression that he held for a long moment. I couldn't tell if the man was angry that he had been caught lying or that Teo himself had led him wrong, but I was relieved when the man rose from the bench and strode off quickly along the bayside without saying a word, his suede boots clicking against the concrete.

"Come on," I said to Teo but he remained leaning against the walkway rail. He didn't move and I was going to have to battle his hardheadedness.

"How'd you get here?" I asked him.

He tilted his chin at the lone car at the opposite side of the road. "That's his LTD," Teo said. "Gold-colored."

It looked just yellow to me. "I meant to Corpus."

"I hitched," he said. "It's not far." Now that the older man was gone, he was back to the Teo I knew, his voice a shield, a tool he could work to his advantage. I could see what the older man had spotted in him and I was torn by what it suggested. His face was too boyish to know anything, which was precisely what had drawn the older man. He wore a white jersey with the number twelve across his thin chest, his best—his only—pair of jeans. I could smell the sour on him, his armpits pungent whenever he moved.

"You can't be here like this," I said. I followed his eyes to where he was looking, the older man long gone. I didn't know where Teo had slept the previous night or how he had met that man, but I didn't want my brother to be in the world that way. Yet I also knew that he had discovered something, a power in his slender frame and his black hair sharp and beautiful in a ragged cut along his nape.

"I don't want to stay in that town," Teo said.

"You won't," I told him, and I hoped that he couldn't hear how I could only picture Mathis for myself, being content with some version of what my parents had. I didn't want to say any more, in case he could hear me lying, but Teo had gone back into a listless, bored look. I was the least on his mind.

"You have to do this right," I said, surprised that I was offering advice. He'd given himself a new name, after all, already figuring out how to protect this new self. He frightened me, in a way, my brother not really my brother, the gold LTD gleaming in the distance. "You need some money in your pocket. You have to work."

Teo didn't answer, but then let out a scoff. "Where are *you* going to work? You're the one who's graduating."

I didn't answer him and was about to say something sharp about it being none of his business, but we both knew that our parents wouldn't pressure me to get a job just yet. Something pleased them about me not having a boyfriend. Now even school couldn't keep me from staying home like they thought a girl should. Teo was younger, but he understood that this was exactly what they wanted until I found a man to marry. His knowledge of their intentions made me feel naive in front of him, as if that older man had shared with him a whole lifetime of questions designed to turn him away from everything that had shaped him.

"I can't promise you I won't leave," Teo said. "I can't be myself there."

"Pick a different name, though," I said. "Teddy? Too white."

Teo's face stiffened a bit. He didn't like being criticized. "I think it fits me."

This was what he wanted and the sister part of me could only console him. "Fine," I agreed. "But don't use it at home. I have to make them believe that you were hungover somewhere and that's enough to handle for a day."

He relaxed when we got in our father's truck and I could tell that he was more tired than he was letting on. Teo rolled down the window, listless in the heat, and I thought of him wandering the streets at night and the solace and allure of someone's air-conditioned car. "Can we make a deal?" I asked. "Wherever you go, send me a postcard with an address where I can find you. I don't want to be wondering."

Teo didn't say yes or no. We got home to our mother's scolding and her following him from room to room and her insistence that he leave his bedroom door open. He weathered the worst of it and settled into expectations. He soon found a job for the summer before I did, a bagging clerk at the tiendita that was walking distance from our house. It pleased our mother that she could literally stand on the porch and watch him make his way to the grocery store and stand there again on punchout. This was false hope, I wanted to tell her. This wasn't the way it was going to be. I knew it when, about a month into the job, Teo silently gave our parents a small portion of his paycheck. Not more than a few dollars and they hadn't even asked, but the gesture softened them, fooled them into thinking he had uncovered a responsible side of himself.

By then, I'd found a full-time job at the five-and-dime that my mother liked to go to. Out of the house, I couldn't follow what Teo did or didn't do, and I kept expecting to come home to find out that he'd gone once again. But that summer went by without incident and when school started, the old routine really did seem to settle our family down. Everyone left in the morning except our mother and by early evening, something was on the stove and served hot as soon as my father got home. We all moved as if by instinct and the routine soothed me. I didn't let it bother me too much that I never saw Teo with books from school or even a packet of worksheets. I hadn't been much of a student myself, sharp but distracted.

We were set on paths. I felt a new duty to simply see Teo through graduation. I had promised nothing and yet I was fired by an obligation, a belief that if he saw how much care and love for him was in our home, he would change his mind about leaving. I was fooled by the quiet of school. He never mentioned problems but that didn't mean they had suddenly stopped. This would occur to me, reaching for the bottom shelf of the workstation, where the store owner kept precious yards of organza and linen for the two rich ladies in town. Dissatisfied with what was on offer, they asked to see what was below the counter. Not everything had to be visible to be possible. I brought the fabric bolts out, as the store owner had shown me, and patiently let them inspect the material, putting them away again if they declined. I watched their faces when they refused, the satisfaction they enjoyed in being able to choose only the exact thing they wanted.

I turned this over and over in my head, especially in the duller hours after lunch. Mornings ran busy, the store serving a loyal circle of older women who completed their errands before noon. I imagined how Teo's mornings might have dragged in comparison to mine and when the afternoons turned hazy with boredom, I thought I felt a bit of what drove his impatience. What would it take to leave the store and not come back tomorrow? What would I miss if I measured time only by Teo being in school?

One afternoon in October, a boy my age came into the store.

He paced the aisles, bewildered by the embroidery thread choices once he found them. "It's for my grandmother," he said, when I approached to help him. "She sent me for dark blue." He handed over the torn label that he'd been given as a guide and I matched it for him. He was sweet and bumbling with the money. I didn't recognize him from school and I told him so.

"I'm here taking care of my grandparents," he said. "I'm from San Antonio." He folded the paper bag with the embroidery thread over and over again in his hands and it was compact and tiny by the time he asked if he could wait for me after work for a soda. It struck me as old-fashioned and fussy, yet right away I could hear my parents objecting, raising questions about who he was and what he wanted. My life wasn't my own, not even for something as simple as a soda.

"Okay," I told him, knowing I would have to be quick, inventing a small lie about being held over at the store. Goyo was waiting for me across the street when I clocked out, standing by a truck just like my father's. He didn't have my father's rounded and thick shoulders, but he was tall and stood straight. He was lanky, his teeth crooked, his clothes pressed, and he was content with walking me to the drugstore across the street for the soda he promised.

We stood on the sidewalk, each with a bottle in hand. I knew any of the passing cars might spot me and people would have a story to tell my parents if they wanted. I let the worry slip and tried to give Goyo a look that meant he didn't have to rush as he told me about being the one in his family who had been called upon to care for his elders. He drove down to Mathis from San Antonio and spent half of the week with them, the rest of the time back in the city at his part-time job. "They need looking after," he said. "It's my grandfather, really. He fell down in his tomato plants one morning and my grandmother couldn't get him up, so now I'm here to do their housework and leave some food to warm up over the weekend."

How long he would have to do this wasn't my business to ask, but I admired him and understood him better for it. I liked that he answered to obligation and that he was probably favored by his grandparents. The older women who came into the shop were often sharp-tongued and demanding, but I could imagine them softening around Goyo, eager to get a graceful, crooked smile out of him.

"I have to go," I said, though it hadn't been more than twenty minutes.

He offered me a ride home, but it was close enough to walk and if I hurried, I could get by with a small lie that I had late inventory to count.

"Can I meet you tomorrow?" he asked.

"Only if it's like today," I answered. "I'm expected to be home right after work."

The look on Goyo's face meant that I didn't have to explain. "Okay," he agreed. "But day after tomorrow, I go to San Antonio for my weekend hours. I really want to see you."

That night, I got no questions from my mother about getting home late and we all sat down to a quick but distracted dinner. A late soccer game was on TV and my father kept glancing up at it between bites. Teo kept his head down. On any other day, I might have felt ignored, but I welcomed a lack of scrutiny. I felt it all over my face, the thinking about Goyo and who he was and how I might get to know him. Before Teo left the table, I even thought I understood why he wanted to leave town so badly. There was no place I could think of in town where I could be out and not be seen by someone.

I lay in bed that night finding myself dreaming of San Antonio, though I had never been there, and I filled it with wider, greener streets than the ones I had driven while searching for Teo in Corpus. Even the garden where Goyo's grandfather had fallen wasn't in Mathis but in San Antonio; it sharpened in my mind as a tidy, neat space with long rows of vegetables, not a weed to be found. I took a certain pride in my heart's focus on places—the city, the streets, and garden—and it let me rest well. It wasn't that I refused to think of Goyo's handsomeness, but that I didn't dwell on it. My frame of mind let me imagine a new place first, how I might want to see something other than Mathis.

Goyo met me the next day as he had promised. All morning, I had fumbled through my tasks, miscounting change badly enough that I had to start over. Each time someone came in, the clock seemed to slow. I had to focus on the customer and couldn't look out to the street, hoping to glimpse Goyo driving by. I told him so when I took the first sip.

Goyo shook his head. "I spent all day with my grandparents," he said, though it wasn't offered as an apology. He had duties and I could tell he expected a lot of himself to meet what others needed from him. "I did tell my grandmother that I was coming to see you," he said. "I think it helps that she knows you work here."

"So she remembers me?"

"She says she does. She says you're a good girl. Are you?"

"Too good," I said, but as soon as I said it, I didn't quite know what I meant. I wanted it to be like Goyo's declaration of how he had spent his day—matter-of-fact and with the certainty of innocence behind it—but I could hear my new frustration. I couldn't lie about not being quite ready to tell my parents.

"My grandparents are the Escobedos, if that helps." I knew what he was trying to do, that maybe saying something about where he came from might ease my parents' questions. But he wasn't in a hurry to convince me of anything. "I've got sisters, too," Goyo said, "but I'm the one who's taking care of my grandparents. I mean—" he hesitated—"I understand what they expect of you as a young lady and me as young man and, I don't know . . . Don't take this the wrong way, but I'm not looking to get married or anything."

I laughed because I knew what he meant and because it was a

relief. The slow stream of questions from my parents would flow in only one direction and any answer short of that path meant that a boy like him would be up to no good. They were closed in and narrow and I laughed at my new clarity, a nervousness with how to deal with it now that I knew.

"Who will take care of you?" I asked, which was my mother's question always, and I could hear in it now what she thought marriage was for.

"I don't want anybody to take care of me," said Goyo. "And I don't want to take care of anybody. I've done that all my life and it won't stop for a long time. Besides, I don't think that's the point of marriage."

I nodded, my soda finished, and I handed him the bottle. The practical older sister came out of me. "Right, but who will take care of you, all the way at the end?"

"Me," Goyo said, direct and confident, full of assurance.

"What about kids? You're going to want kids to take care of you in the end."

"No," Goyo said. "Just me. I mean it." He took the bottle from me and placed it in a cardboard box in the back of the truck, where he was saving them for return. "I don't believe I have to answer to anybody. Not even God. When I get old—too old—I'll go right up to the edge of the Gulf and walk straight in."

Later that night, I wondered why Goyo's words didn't scare me. I didn't know him at all and yet I didn't doubt his sincerity. I thought of the man who had picked up my brother and how he'd gone off along the edge of the bay. *When I get old*, I heard Goyo's voice say again and again, and I imagined that man slipping into the deep, still water. At the dinner table with my mother's bowed head and my father's distracted gaze at the television, I knew Goyo didn't mean it as any kind of dark wish. Teo would understand and I thought of telling him. He might understand what kind of person Goyo was.

But by the time we had finished eating, Teo still hadn't come home and the plate my mother left covered in foil for him on the stove cooled. "No lo entiendo," my mother said, exasperated.

He had his reasons, I knew, the deep ones that haunted him, but I couldn't help wonder that maybe he had seen me on the street with Goyo. He knew I would soon be distracted with my parents' judgment and this was a chance to slip away. Shame seeped into me for imagining this, but anger, too. I could see what Goyo meant now by his sisters, the void that needed to be filled when family didn't act like it was supposed to.

In the morning, I rose early and did the cooking, much to my mother's surprise. I knew they would think I was getting ready to go find Teo, but I lingered over the coffee and then cleaned the dishes without rushing. I wanted them to ask me directly about my brother. I wanted them to take some responsibility for what they knew about why he left. If they knew his heart, I thought, maybe they would know mine.

"I don't know where he is this time," I said, suspecting that Teo wouldn't have gone back to the same place twice. "I'm working now. I can't mind his business anymore." My mother sighed and called our tía, though he hadn't been hanging out with our cousins at all, and when she hung up the phone, she sat heavily at the table and looked at me.

"Cuando le falta dinero," my father said, "se le acaba este pedo." But he didn't know how my brother could solve a money problem if he needed to.

Every boy who ran from his family was somehow wrapped up in drugs, my tía said later, when she came over to comfort my mother. His room should have been searched a long time ago, but it was too late now. My mother named the people she thought were his friends. The two of them sat in the kitchen and counted out all the ways in which my mother had missed the signs. It took everything I had to not disagree with them. I didn't want my mother to think that I might know more than I did.

All weekend, I was torn by my mother's stricken face. She looked genuinely confused about Teo running off and I seized at the thought that this bewilderment might turn quickly to resentment if I didn't help steer her toward calm. I wanted to tell her about Goyo, now that I realized what it meant for your ideas to change once someone burrowed themselves into your mind.

"If he promised that he'd write to you," Goyo said, when we saw each other a few days later, "why don't you trust him to do that?" I'd spilled what had happened almost from the moment of approaching his truck. I had a story to tell him now and I was the one who suggested we go to the burger joint on the other side of the small downtown. I wasn't minding the time, but I was eased by Goyo's attention—I could tell he was listening to me, but that he wouldn't be quick to offer help. My problems were my own and his look told me that I had the strength to solve them.

"I don't have any jotos in my family—"

"Don't call him that. I don't like that word."

"That's what he is."

"He's my little brother," I said. "He's only sixteen."

Goyo quieted. I knew he was sorry, but he wouldn't apologize. "All I mean is that I understand why he can't be in a town this small and not go crazy. I know he's young, but he'll do all right for himself."

"He thinks he's grown up . . ." I said.

"Didn't you think that? When you thought you could figure everything out? My grandparents came up from Mexico when they were thirteen or fourteen. When you don't have anything, you get smart."

"Those were different times," I said. Then I said it again because I needed to hear it for myself.

"He'll be fine," Goyo assured me.

I let Goyo drive me home but there wasn't as much as a curtain flick when he pulled up to the house. It surprised me and I couldn't tell if my mother, always alert, was just pretending that she hadn't heard the truck. I entered the house with no one asking why I was late and the longer the quiet went on, a new sense deepened. What happened to Teo meant more to them than what happened to me.

It angered me when I realized this and when my mother announced that dinner was ready, I told them that I had already eaten. I let them stay in their silence. I sat in the living room, not bothering to change the channel from the local news. Their forks clattered as they ate dinner quickly and when my father returned to the living room, I went back into the kitchen and helped my mother clean. She didn't refuse my help and maybe she wanted me to see that she had made enough food not only for me but also for Teo. I wondered when she would stop doing that, how soon she'd turn practical and full of a sudden, tougher love.

"¿Quién es?" she asked softly, both of us by the sink. She let the water run, I saw, so my father wouldn't hear.

"Es el nieto de Doña Escobedo." I didn't say more, but she didn't push for anything else. She handed me dish after dish and we worked together in a way that lifted my fog of anger. She knew more than I thought, and maybe it was my father she didn't want to be stirred with too much knowledge. Maybe it was the best way to let Teo go.

Later that night, all the lights down and my father already in bed, my mother came up behind me as I brushed my teeth at the bathroom sink. She touched my shoulder briefly, a surprise in itself as a way to say good night, and it was only when she had already turned back to their room that I saw the small velvet box she had slipped onto the corner of the sink counter. Inside, a small pendant necklace from my Avon-selling tía, a gold heart leaning to one side as if being blown down by the wind, a speck of purple stone that was meant to be amethyst. It was already too late to thank her, the door to the room closed, but I slept with the velvet box underneath my pillow, and in the morning we all carried on as normal.

I wore the necklace as a kind of permission and I held it as my mother's trust that I wouldn't stray off with Goyo. She was asking something of me now, knowing my brother wouldn't be back. Goyo complimented me on the necklace when he saw it, feathering the gold heart briefly with two fingertips. He let it go gently, nonchalant as in everything he did, and it startled me—not just his touch, but my response, electric and feverish, my mind already spinning around whether or not this was what falling in love was all about. It made me tell Goyo the story of how my mother had given it to me and he searched my face for what it meant.

"She trusts you," he said. "That's a good thing."

"I don't like the word 'trust.' It makes it sound like it was something she decided to do just that day."

"There's a lot of words you don't like," said Goyo.

"I'm being serious. Trust is a test, don't you think?"

"Absolutely," he said, coolly and quick.

We carried on for a while, nearly every day at the end of work and his weekends taking him back to San Antonio. Sometimes we would drive out to the edge of the lake on the west side of town and his sweet side would go quiet, our eyes closed and our hands roaming. It felt good to be like that with him, how natural and unhurried it was. A sadness sometimes came over me, thinking of my brother in the gold LTD, and I'd press my face deeper into Goyo's shoulder. He never mistook this for encouragement—we never went very far— and I was grateful that he let our emotions still the air between us. We didn't have to name what we were feeling.

One day a postcard arrived and I caught it before either of my parents sorted through the mail. "Bea," it read, in the tiniest handwriting all around the entire edge, "come get me." I had to squint to read the address Teo had etched along the border. The picture showed the San Antonio River Walk, an outdoor restaurant with orange and yellow umbrellas tilted for shade. I showed the card to Goyo the next time I met him and he flipped it quickly after he saw the picture.

"He's in a nice neighborhood."

"You know where it is?"

"More or less."

"What would you think about taking me there?"

Goyo looked down at the card, returning to the restaurant scene. "You know, I always wanted to eat at one of those places."

"Will you?" I asked. "This weekend when you go back?"

"I'm working . . ." he said. I couldn't think of what to say to this, no matter how obvious and true it was. He had his responsibilities and I had mine.

"Is he in trouble? What does he mean?"

"I just want to go get him. I figured since you know the city . . ."

It was a Thursday and he went back on Fridays usually. "We can go tonight if you want to," Goyo offered, "and we can come back late. That way I don't risk missing hours."

I was bothered about telling my parents that I would be driving into San Antonio with Goyo, who they had yet to meet. I wondered if I should tell them anything at all, whether it was worth it to worry them a little if I simply brought Teo in tow. I reached out to take the card back from Goyo, looking at it once more as if a new clue would help me sort myself out.

"Tomorrow is too hard," Goyo said, as if sensing that I thought I had options. "I can't miss work hours."

"Okay," I said. "Let's go."

The farther we got from Mathis, the worse I felt. Even if I did come back with Teo, a certain damage would be done in my mother's imagination. My absence would confirm what she always knew I would do and I could see my tía coming over to say exactly the same thing. I said little to Goyo on the drive as we sped along the highway but he seemed unbothered by my lack of conversation. I had a stronger appreciation for what he was doing for me. Small talk couldn't carry me past how guilty I felt for asking this of him.

Goyo drove us out in a kind of smooth rush, passing car after car but not speeding, a different caution than my father's. By the time we hit the outskirts of San Antonio, it was too dark for me to make anything out, but Goyo's familiarity guided him along the streets and he stopped in front of a two-story house, a small balcony at the top where I pictured Teo leaning out in wait.

"I'll come with you," Goyo said, as I sat in the passenger seat, looking up at the house. He got out of the truck and I double-checked the address to be sure it was the right place, the house so big that I couldn't believe my brother would want to leave it.

I half-expected the man in the gold LTD to answer the door, but this man was thinner, his hair like faded bronze. He was dressed neatly in a shirt and tie, as if he had just gotten home from an important job. "Can I help you?"

"Is Teddy here?"

"Teddy," the man said flatly. He looked at Goyo and then back at me, his face hardening between glances. He half-shut the door, but placed his hand up to us, a gesture to wait. I saw him climb the shiny brown stairs that led up toward the room with the balcony and after a quiet pause, we could hear one voice rise, then another. It was Teo, I knew, his mean voice, but he didn't speak long. It was the older man who kept asking questions and they floated away unanswered over Teo's footsteps.

He came down the stairs holding a satchel I had never seen before and he looked surprised to see Goyo. "Who are you?" he asked, stepping past the threshold without really waiting to hear either one of us.

Goyo put his hands out to stop him. "I'm your ride home," he said, not sternly but firm enough that Teo had to catch my eye.

As Goyo led us back to the truck, I kept waiting for the older man to come down the stairs. Teo had left the door open behind him and this would be the moment, I was certain, when the man would come bounding out after him.

But no such thing happened. Teo climbed into the bed of the truck but Goyo immediately told him no. "Up front," he said. "You wouldn't like it back there on the highway going real fast." I slid into the middle of the bench seat and Teo climbed in beside me, staring out at the big house with its front door open like a mouth with nothing to say.

Goyo drove us out of the neighborhood, the windows warm and yellow. It had grown too dark for me to see anything but the lights of the city and then a bit of rain started to fall. Without saying anything, Goyo pulled over to grab the satchel that Teo had left in the back and we started back to the highway. In the quiet of the truck cab, in some other circumstance, I would have liked the gentle hiss of the tires over the wet road and the green traffic lights glowing against the pavement. I would've liked to peer out of the window without blinking and take in the newness of a city I didn't know. But all I felt was shame for why we'd come to save Teo.

"So how did you know that man?" Goyo ventured, once we truly were out among the smaller towns.

"He paid me money to fuck me up the ass," Teo said.

"Teo!" I snapped. "You don't need to be talking like that."

"It's no one's business to be asking about my life," Teo said. He had his head turned out to the edge of the highway, a conversation he really didn't want to have.

"I wasn't trying to get in your business," Goyo said. "I just think you owe it to your sister to tell her what's up."

"Nobody has to ask anybody questions about things they already know," Teo replied. "I know you're Bea's boyfriend just by looking at you. Why do I have to know how that happened?"

"All right," I said. "All right." We went the rest of the way in a tense quiet, the rain following us along. When we pulled up to the house, Teo stepped out of the truck even before it stopped, the truck door open like the rich man's house in San Antonio.

Goyo didn't shift into park. I had been preparing for the truck to stop, to be turned off, for him to walk up with me to the steps of the house, and to introduce him to my parents. If they only knew who had helped get Teo back . . .

"It's not my place to say, but I'm sorry to tell you that your brother is going to drag you down someday."

"He's got a smart mouth . . ." I started.

"I don't mean talking back," Goyo said. "I mean that you're never going to know a moment's peace in your life if you keep cleaning up his messes."

I looked at the house, at the windows lit but not warm, and I could hear my mother's exasperation even over the sound of Goyo's truck. He wasn't going to turn off the engine.

"You're not going to come see me again, are you?" I asked.

Goyo sighed. I thought maybe he really was thinking it over, but I saw now for the first time that he was struggling with staying true to himself. I knew what he wanted to say. Part of me was touched that he found it so hard to do. An angrier side of me wanted to make him say it.

"We each have our own roads," he said.

I scrambled out of the truck, the words burning behind me. My eyes welled even before I made it to the front door. I wanted to blur into the night somehow. Goyo's truck stayed rumbling in the street but I was too crushed to turn around. I knew he wasn't waiting for me to come back. He was waiting for me to go inside safely, the way his parents raised him, and once I went past the door, that would be it. I'd float into my next world, aimless, and the only thing guiding me would be the tightened anger in my family's voice. I stepped inside the house and I slipped under the voices bubbling around me, their arguing an echo I couldn't figure out anymore. "I don't know," I said to whatever my mother was asking me, putting up my hands. My head pounded and my feet felt like they'd lost contact with the ground. "I don't know."

All night, I couldn't sleep. I felt divided against myself, one moment convinced that Goyo didn't really mean what he said, then all but certain he possessed a reserve that I had underestimated. He had told me all along that he didn't want to take care of anyone. It seemed right, then, that he would mean this about Teo as well. It didn't matter to him if Teo was too young to know any better.

In the morning, I let my parents sort it out with Teo, but there was nothing to solve. The tiendita job that he'd left would be hard to get again but he was under orders to go down to the store and beg. Teo made a grudging promise that he would and he put on a responsible show again, bringing his soiled clothes from the satchel and washing them by hand. I watched out the back window as he strung the clothesline with colorful shirts, one after the other, unmistakable in their expensive loudness. He's leaving as soon as they dry, I thought to myself, but I didn't care if he did or not.

I looked up at the bright sky, the previous night's rain long gone, and promised the sun that I wouldn't ever pull Teo out of a rut again if I could just have Goyo be an angel with me once more. I wished him some peace over the weekend, away from his duties with his grandparents, away from this little town with nothing in it. My pride caught in my throat. Monday, I thought. He'll come by the store on Monday.

I spent the rest of weekend in a kind of haze. I was impatient and testy, but I had nowhere to go when I felt drowned out by the bickering over Teo. By Saturday evening, my tía arrived to listen to my mother's complaints and Teo sat out in the backyard rather than hear any of it. "Mija," my tía said to me, since there was no one else who was capable of listening, "the Bible says you have to be your brother's keeper."

"Ni van a la iglesia," said my father. "Muy pinches cristianos en esta casa . . ."

They turned on each other for a moment, my father railing against the church, my mother and my tía insisting that not going to church was exactly why we were the way we were. She turned to me again, my tía, as my parents sniped at each other. "You see why you have to take care of your brother?"

I understood that I would have to. But I didn't understand why I had to. It made sense to me now what Goyo was so dead set against and I knew that, on Monday at the end of the workday, he would not show up.

And that was exactly what happened. I could see the empty street from my position at the sales counter and I didn't linger. I didn't turn this way and that looking for Goyo's truck. I went straight home. I said nothing at dinner as my mother kept going round about Teo. I wanted her to ask about Goyo. I wanted her to notice. I wanted the chance to tell the truth about him. I wanted the chance to tell her that I had lost something too.

I rehearsed it in my mind: I think I fell in love, I would tell her. And what did she think about someone who thought you owed nobody nothing, not even the person you married? Was that enough?

But the next day, the satchel and the colorful shirts were gone, and my mother slipped under the wave of missing Teo. If I wanted to imagine my life out loud, no one would hear it. As long as Teo was gone, nothing else would matter. It became as clear and obvious to me as sunlight.

I kept thinking of the times when I could have moved back toward what I thought I wanted. It reminded me of being on the Gulf shore when I was twelve and staring out at a dark speck on the horizon, certain that it was a boat getting closer, before it all faded out to nothing.

The days became the same. I knew where the Escobedos lived but

I flattered myself that I wouldn't beg for Goyo. The weeks stretched and became months. I drove to Houston one time after a postcard came and I waited for Teo at a dingy two-story apartment complex. A brutal-looking man stood only in shorts at the top of the stairs and he followed Teo all the way down to my father's truck. He reached into the truck cab as we were pulling away and smashed Teo's head into the dashboard. Teo left our house again before the deep bruise over his right eye had even healed. My father's eyesight failed slowly and I sat with him in the orange plastic chairs in the Corpus Christi state offices and realized, for the first time, that he had never understood half of the state papers he had been asked to sign in the past. At the five-and-dime, fewer and fewer of the old ladies came in to shop. There would be no one to replace them. My mother's left hand started to gnarl at the knuckles with arthritis and I found myself cooking for them after work. Word reached us that Don Escobedo passed away. Then, not two months later, la doña. "The ones who are really in love always go in pairs," my mother said.

I drove by the Escobedo house just once, certain that I'd see Goyo there clearing out the place, but it was already empty. Even the yard had been trimmed back at every possible point, the tomato plants gone, the windows vacant. I wasn't ever going to see him again.

Sometimes I'd drive by the Escobedo house and I'd see children in the yard. A family lived there now, the adults sitting out front on the hot evenings. Now that his grandparents were gone, I wondered if Goyo had softened some. Maybe now he had met someone and maybe now he was married. Maybe now he was ready to be more giving. But people don't change, I know. Not one person I knew had ever wavered from how they saw the world. Not Teo. Not my father or mother. Not Goyo. Not me. I would be taking care of everyone until the day they were all gone, and I had a hard time, some days, accepting whether I chose to do that or if this was the way it was always supposed to be.

It made me hate Teo, not long after that, when he asked me for a ride out of Corpus Christi. He left a man in tears, the first time I ever thought that maybe love could have happened for him, but it was easy for him to get in the truck and find another way to start over. I swore it would be the last time that I would ever do this for him, but then came a man in Brownsville and then another in Houston and then back to Corpus. He looked older than he needed to be every time. Not once, though, did he ever send me a postcard from San Antonio.

It went on like this for a long time. I gave up the job at the five-and-dime the year that Teo sent me a postcard from California. A brittle, yellowed card of people picking oranges, FRESNO in block letters underneath. *Please*, Teo had written, something he had not ever written before. The word frightened me some, how young and helpless it sounded. I thought about it for a day before I took some savings and bought a Greyhound ticket. What did it matter, I thought, with the five-and-dime ready to close before year's end? What was left for me? I could start over when I got back. My mother was alarmed at the suitcase and I lied to them, saying I was going to Dallas. Far was far, but I didn't want to let on that I was going all the way to California. I thought they would stop me from going and I wanted the long trip back. I wanted to explain to Teo why this was the last time and that I would never be a fool again.

I felt less sure the longer the trip lasted. The hours pressed on and as the lowlands gave way to the desert, I knew I'd gone out too far this time. There was no going back. The bus took me deeper into places I didn't recognize, not even from movies, and I pictured how Goyo might be fearless in the face of it. In spite of myself, at my loneliest, he was always with me. I stared out of the windows at the dark mountains and wondered if he would have stayed had I refused my brother. I decided nothing fair had ever been asked of me by anyone and by the time I pulled into the station at Los Angeles, days later, I knew. Nighttime had already fallen at our arrival, but the station bustled. I bought a cup of coffee and sat on one of the benches and watched people go by. A woman in a purple dress and white shoes hustled by, pulled along by her sister. She looked reluctant to go wherever they were headed. Part of me wanted to reach out to stop her, to tell her to stay, to do what she wanted, but her sister was strong and they slipped out into the Los Angeles night. I heard an announcement for San Diego, another for Santa Barbara. When the call for Fresno came, I knew then that I wasn't going to move. I let it pass over me like a wave. Teo would figure out that I wasn't coming for him after all. I was in sudden awe of myself for relying on luck, and my hand went up to the necklace my mother had gifted me, as if the amethyst had an answer, for me and Teo both. When the Fresno bus left, I thought the station would quiet like someone letting out a long sigh of relief, but it was as busy as ever. Life went on, a small mercy. I finished my coffee and sat at the bench with the empty cup in my hand. I could see a bit of the city I didn't know every time the bus station doors opened and closed. The lights came through, shimmered from someplace way out there. I knew there were more lights beyond that, deeper and deeper, and it wasn't but a little while before I gathered my courage and waded out into them.

ACKNOWLEDGMENTS

My gratitude to the many editors who published earlier versions of these stories and whose support of my work kept me going in times of great doubt: "Anyone Can Do It" in *ZYZZYVA, The Best American Short Stories 2019*, and *The Penguin Book of the Modern American Short Story*; "The Happiest Girl in the Whole USA" in *Glimmer Train Stories* and *The O. Henry Prize Stories 2015*; "Presumido" in *Huizache: The Magazine of Latino Literature*; "Susto" in *Freeman's: The Best New Writing on California*; "The Reason Is Because" in *American Short Fiction* and *The O. Henry Prize Stories 2017*; "The Consequences" in *Southwest Review*; "That Pink House at the End of the Street on the Other Side of Town" in *Virginia Quarterly Review*. Portions of "Fieldwork" appeared as "Fieldwork" in *Tales of Two Americas: Stories of Inequality in a Divided Nation* and as "La Pura Verdad" in *Territory*.

Special gracias to Laura Furman, John Freeman, Heidi Pitlor, and Anthony Doerr for placing my Valley stories into new conversations. Much appreciation to Susan Burmeister-Brown and Linda B. Swanson-Davies, who gave me my first big break so many years ago, and whose much-missed *Glimmer Train Stories* was a beacon to all of us in love with cuentos. Sara Reggiani of Edizioni Black Coffee, whose early enthusiasm was an important factor in getting me to realize I was closer to a book than I believed: grazie.

Ethan Nosowsky, gracias for editing these stories with a big-hearted respect for the people and the place I love so much, as well as to Susie Nicklin of The Indigo Press for such care and assistance. Thank you to Anni Liu, Katie Dublinski, Marisa Atkinson, Claudia Acevedos-Quiñones, and everyone at Graywolf for guiding this book into the light and making me feel like a writer again.

For their curiosity and inspiring consejos: Sandra Cisneros, Cherríe Moraga, Virginia Grise, Rafael Pérez-Torres, and Joan Soble. For still listening when my voice dropped quiet: Ken Stuckey, Aaron Smith, and Curt Weber. For their embracing spirits, consummate guidance, and encouragement: Alison Hawthorne Deming, Aurelie Sheehan, Adela Licona, Jamie Lee, and Jane Miller. The circle who sustained me in the desert: gracias always to Megan Campbell, Allison Dushane, Paul Hurh, Clint McCall, Ander Monson, and Jon Reinhardt. For never once doubting me, even when I doubted myself: my agent Stuart Bernstein. The ever-bright star to me and many: Helena María Viramontes.

I was graced by my parents with long-held cuentos that served as inspiration for some stories in this book. I remain in awe of their lives and how the long roads of their survival made my life and my writing possible. Finally, I honor the late Donald B. Burroughs, dear friend and mentor, who changed many lives as a beloved high school teacher in Cambridge and as an advocate for literacy and storytelling for all communities: I will see you on the other side of the sky.

Manuel Muñoz is the author of a novel, *What You See in the Dark*, and the short story collections *Zigzagger* and *The Faith Healer of Olive Avenue*, which was shortlisted for the Frank O'Connor International Short Story Award. He is the recipient of fellowships from the National Endowment for the Arts and the New York Foundation for the Arts. He has been recognized with a Whiting Writer's Award, three O. Henry Awards, and an appearance in *Best American Short Stories*.

A native of Dinuba, California, he currently lives and works in Tucson, Arizona.

The text of *The Consequences* is set in Adobe Garamond Pro.
Book design by Rachel Holscher.
Composition by Bookmobile Design and Digital Publisher Services,
Minneapolis, Minnesota.
Manufactured by Versa Press on acid-free,
30 percent postconsumer wastepaper.